D0792796

THE PATIENCE STONE

Born in Afghanistan in 1962, Atiq Rahimi fled to France in 1984. There he has made a name as a writer, film- and documentary-maker of exceptional note. His first novel, *Earth and Ashes*, was widely acclaimed and his film of the book was in the Official Selection at Cannes, 2004. He is adapting his second novel, *A Thousand Rooms of Dream and Fear*, for the screen. Since 2001, he has returned to Afghanistan many times to set up a Writers' House in Kabul and offer support and training to young writers and film-makers. He was the winner of the Goncourt Prize 2008 for *The Patience Stone* (*Syngué sabour*), his first novel to be written in French. He lives in Paris.

ATIQ RAHIMI

The Patience Stone

TRANSLATED FROM THE FRENCH BY
Polly McLean

WITH AN INTRODUCTION BY
Khaled Hosseini

VINTAGE BOOKS
London

Published by Vintage 2011

2 4 6 8 10 9 7 5 3 1

First published in France as *Syngué sabour* by P.O.L éditeur in 2008.

Copyright   P.O.L éditeur, 2008
Translation copyright © Polly McLean 2010
Introduction copyright © Khaled Hosseini 2010

Atiq Rahimi has asserted his right under the Copyright, Designs
and Patents Act 1988 to be identified as the author of this work

Quotes from the Koran taken from *The Koran*, trans. N. J. Dawood
(Penguin Classics 1956, Fifth revised edition 1990).
Copyright © N. J. Dawood, 1956, 1959, 1966, 1968, 1974, 1990,
1993, 1997, 1999, 2003, 2006.
Reprinted by permission of the Penguin Group.

First published in Great Britain in 2010 by
Chatto & Windus

Vintage
Random House, 20 Vauxhall Bridge Road,
London SW1V 2SA

www.vintage-books.co.uk

Addresses for companies within The Random House Group Limited
can be found at: www.randomhouse.co.uk/offices.htm

The Random House Group Limited Reg. No. 954009

A CIP catalogue record for this book
is available from the British Library

ISBN 9780099539544

The Random House Group Limited supports The Forest Stewardship
Council (FSC), the leading international forest certification
organisation. All our titles that are printed on Greenpeace approved
FSC certified paper carry the FSC logo. Our paper procurement
policy can be found at www.rbooks.co.uk/environment

Mixed Sources
Product group from well-managed
forests and other controlled sources
www.fsc.org Cert no. TT-COC-2139
© 1996 Forest Stewardship Council

Printed and bound in Great Britain by
CPI Bookmarque, Croydon, CR0 4TD

This tale, written in memory of N.A. – an Afghan poet savagely murdered by her husband – is dedicated to M.D.

From the body by the body with the body
Since the body and until the body.

Antonin Artaud

Introduction

by

Khaled Hosseini

It is a vexing fact that women are the most belea-guered members of Afghan society. Long before the arrival of the Taliban, Afghan women struggled for basic rights. Outside of a few urban pockets, the ironclad rule of patriarchal, tribal law has long denied women their right to work, education, adequate health care, and personal independence – all of this made infinitely worse by three decades of war, displacement, and anarchy. Though there have been some improvements in recent years, far too many women continue to languish under the unquestioned, absolute domination of tribal customs that deprive them of meaningful participation in societal life. For far too long, Afghan women have been faceless and voiceless.

Until now. With *The Patience Stone*, Atiq Rahimi gives face and voice to one unforgettable woman – and, one could argue, offers her as a proxy for the grievances of millions.

The plot could not be simpler. The entire story unfolds in one room, where an unnamed woman nurses her badly injured husband, who lies motion-less, wordless, and helpless. As warring factions plunder and pillage on the streets, the woman feeds her husband through a tube. She lubricates his eyes and changes him. And she speaks to him. Tentatively at first, until gradually, the dam ruptures, letting loose a flood of startling confessions. With increasing boldness, the woman reveals how she has resented her husband, her disappointments in him, her fiercely guarded secrets, her desires and hopes, the pains and sorrows she has suffered at his hands. As her husband lies before her like a stone – indeed like the legendary titular stone, which absorbs the anguish of all who confess to it – the woman suddenly finds herself free from all restraint and her monologues reach a fevered pitch. What pours out of her is not only a brave and shocking confession, but a savage indictment of war, the brutality of men, and the religious, marital and cultural norms that continually assault Afghan women, leaving them with no recourse but to absorb without complaint, like a patience stone.

It is to Atiq Rahimi's credit that his heroine is no saint suffering quietly in purdah. Nor is she much of a heroine. As the woman's one-way discourse with her presumably unconscious husband goes on, the layers are peeled back, revelations come forth, and what emerges is the portrait of a complex and nuanced human being. Rahimi's heroine is brave, resilient, a devout mother, but she is also flawed in fundamentally human ways, a woman capable of lying, manipulating, of being spiteful, a creature that, pushed hard enough, bares her teeth. And her body. Here, Rahimi has broached a great Afghan taboo: the notion of a woman as a sexual being. A pair of passages in this novel may very well generate protest from the more conservative sectors of the Afghan community, but Rahimi is to be applauded for not shying away from the subject. He is to be commended for not turning his heroine into the archetype of the saintly, asexual, maternal figure. Perhaps, writing this novel in French, and not in Dari, made it easier for him. He has been quoted as saying, '. . . a kind of involuntary self-censorship has come into play when I've written in Persian. My acquired language, the one I have chosen, gives me a kind of freedom to express myself, away from this self-censorship and an unconscious shame that dwells in us from childhood.' Whatever the reason, the reader benefits from his unflinching approach.

It is also a testament to Rahimi's considerable literary skills how vividly the war on the streets is depicted, even though the entire tale unfolds within the confines of a single bedroom. The spectre of the unnamed conflict, fought between never named factions, is the third character in the room. Rahimi chooses to not take us to the streets. Instead, we experience war as most helpless civilians do. We hear the sudden bursts of gunfire, the screams, the terrifying silences. We feel the impact of mortar fire when the room shakes and plaster flakes rain down. Despite never taking us to the streets – or perhaps because of it – Rahimi succeeds in making us experience the chaos, the helplessness, the senseless brutality committed with impunity, the random and sudden outbursts of violence that take unsuspecting lives. The years of factional infighting were some of the darkest of the last thirty years in Afghanistan, and in Rahimi's spare prose, the era comes to life to devastating effect.

The Patience Stone, winner of the prestigious Goncourt Prize in France, is a deceptively simple book, written in a spare, poetic style. But it is a rich read, part allegory, part a tale of retribution, part an exploration of honour, love, sex, marriage, war. It is without doubt an important and courageous book. In this reader's view, though, this novel's greatest achievement is in giving voice. Giving voice to those who, as the fable goes, suffer the most and cry out the least. Rahimi's nameless heroine is a conduit, a living vessel for the grievances of millions of women like her, women who have been objectified, marginalised, scorned, beaten, ridiculed, silenced. In *The Patience Stone*, they have their say at last.

THE PATIENCE STONE

Somewhere in Afghanistan or elsewhere

T HE ROOM is small. Rectangular. Stifling, despite the paleness of the turquoise walls, and the two curtains patterned with migrating birds frozen mid-flight against a yellow and blue sky. Holes in the curtains allow the rays of the sun to reach the faded stripes of a kilim. At the far end of the room is another curtain. Green. Unpatterned. Concealing a disused door. Or an alcove.

The room is bare. Bare of decoration. Except between the two windows where someone has hung a small khanjar on the wall, and above the khanjar a photo of a man with a moustache. He is about thirty years old. Curly hair. Square face, bracketed by a pair of neatly tended sideburns. His black eyes sparkle. They are small, separated by a hawk-like nose. The man is not laughing, and yet seems as if he is holding back a laugh. This gives him a strange expression, that of a man inwardly mocking those

1

who look at him. The photo is in black and white, hand-coloured in drab tones.

Facing this photo, at the foot of a wall, the same man – older now – is lying on a red mattress on the floor. He has a beard. Pepper-and-salt. He is thinner. Too thin. Nothing but skin and bones. Pale. Wrinkled. His nose more hawk-like than ever. He still isn't laughing, and still looks strangely mocking. His mouth is half-open. His eyes, even smaller now, have retreated into their sockets. His gaze is fixed on the ceiling, on the exposed, blackened, rotting beams. His arms lie passive along his sides. Beneath his translucent skin, the veins twine around the jutting bones of his body like sleeping worms. On his left wrist he wears a wind-up watch, and on his ring finger a gold wedding band. A tube drips clear liquid into the crook of his arm from a plastic pouch attached to the wall just above his head. The rest of his body is covered by a long blue shirt, embroidered at the collar and cuffs. His legs, stiff as two stakes, are buried under a white sheet. A dirty white sheet.

A hand, a woman's hand, is resting on his chest, over his heart, rising and falling in time with his breath.

The woman is seated. Knees pulled into her chest. Head sunk between her knees. Her dark hair – it is very dark, and long – covers her slumped shoulders, rising and falling with the regular movement of her arm.

In the other hand, the left, she holds a long string of black prayer beads. She moves them between her fingers, telling them. Silently. Slowly. In time with her shoulders. In time with the man's breath. Her body is swathed in a long dress. Crimson. Embroidered, at the cuffs and bottom hem, with a few discreet ears and flowers of corn.

Within reach, open at the flyleaf and placed on a velvet pillow, is a book, the Koran.

A little girl is crying. She is not in the room. Perhaps she's next door. Or in the passage.

The woman's head moves. Wearily. Emerges from the crook of her knees.

The woman is beautiful. At the crease of her left eye, a small scar narrows the place where the eyelids meet, lending a strange wariness to her gaze. Her plump, dry, pale lips are softly and slowly repeating the same word of prayer.

A second little girl starts crying. She seems closer than the first, probably just behind the door.

The woman removes her hand from the man's chest. She stands up and leaves the room. Her absence doesn't change a thing. The man still does not move. He continues to breathe silently, slowly.

The sound of the woman's footsteps quietens the two children. She stays with them for some time, until the house and the world become mere shadows in their sleep; then she returns. In one hand, a small white bottle, in the other, the black prayer beads. She sits down next to the man, opens the bottle, leans over and administers two drops into his right eye, two into his left. Without letting go of her prayer beads. Without pausing in her telling of them.

The rays of the sun shine through the holes in the yellow and blue sky of the curtains, caressing the woman's back and her shoulders as they continue to rock to the rhythm of the prayer beads passing between her fingers.

Far away, somewhere in the city, a bomb explodes. The violence destroys a few houses perhaps, a few dreams. There's a counter attack. The retaliations tear through the heavy midday silence, shaking the window panes but not waking the children. For a

4

moment – just two prayer beads – the woman's shoulders stop moving. She puts the bottle of eye-drops in her pocket. Murmurs '*Al-Qahhar*'. Repeats '*Al-Qahhar*'. Repeats it each time the man takes a breath. And with every repetition, slips one of the prayer beads through her fingers.

One cycle of the prayer beads is complete. Ninety-nine beads. Ninety-nine times '*Al-Qahhar*'.

She sits up and returns to her place on the mattress, next to the man's head, and puts her right hand back on his chest. Begins another cycle of the prayer beads.

As she again reaches the ninety-ninth '*Al-Qahhar*', her hand leaves the man's chest and travels towards his neck. Her fingers wander into the bushy beard, resting there for one or two breaths, emerging to pause a moment on the lips, stroke the nose, the eyes, the brow, and finally vanish again, into the thickness of the filthy hair. 'Can you feel my hand?' She leans over him, straining, and stares into his eyes. No response. She bends her ear to his lips. No sound. Just the same unsettling expression, mouth half-open, gaze lost in the dark beams of the ceiling.

5

She bends down again to whisper, 'In the name of Allah, give me a sign to let me know that you feel my hand, that you're alive, that you'll come back to me, to us! Just a sign, a little sign to give me strength, and faith.' Her lips tremble. They beg, 'Just a word . . .', as they brush lightly over the man's ear. 'I hope you can hear me, at least.' She lays her head on the pillow.

'They told me that after two weeks you'd be able to move, to respond . . . But this is the third week, or nearly. And still nothing!' Her body shifts so she is lying on her back. Her gaze wanders, joining his vacant gaze somewhere among the dark and rotting beams.

'Al-Qahhar, Al-Qahhar, Al-Qahhar . . .'

The woman sits up slowly. Stares desperately at the man. Puts her hand back on his chest. 'If you can breathe, you must be able to hold your breath, surely? Hold it!' Pushing her hair back behind her shoulders, she repeats, 'Hold it, just once!' and again bends her ear to his mouth. She listens. She hears him. He is breathing.

In despair, she mutters, 'I can't take it any more.'

With an angry sigh, she suddenly stands up and repeats, shouting: 'I can't take it any more . . .' Then more dejected: 'Reciting the names of God, over and over from dusk till dawn, I just can't take it!' She moves a few steps closer to the photo, without looking at it. 'It's been sixteen days . . .' She hesitates. 'No . . .', counting on her fingers, unsure.

Confused, she turns around, returns to her spot and glances at the open page of the Koran. Checks. 'Sixteen days . . . so today it's the sixteenth name of God that I'm supposed to chant. *Al-Qahhar*, the Dominant. Yes, that's right, that is the sixteenth name . . .' Thoughtful: 'Sixteen days!' She takes a step back. 'Sixteen days that I've been existing in time with your breath.' Hostile: 'Sixteen days that I've been breathing with you!' She stares at the man. 'Look, I breathe just like you!' She takes a deep breath in, exhales it laboriously. In time with him. 'Even without my hand on your chest, I still breathe like you.' She bends over him. 'And even when I'm not near you, I still breathe in time with you.' She backs away from him. 'Do you hear me?' She starts shouting '*Al-Qahhar*', and telling the prayer beads again, still to the same rhythm. She walks out of the room. We hear her shouting,

7

'*Al-Qahhar, Al-Qahhar* . . .' in the passage and beyond . . .

'*Al-Qahhar* . . .' moves away.
    '*Al-Qahhar* . . .' becomes faint.
    '*Al* . . .' Imperceptible.
    Is gone.

A few moments drift by in silence. Then '*Al-Qahhar*' returns, audible through the window, from the passage, from behind the door. The woman comes back into the room and stops next to the man. Standing. Her left hand still telling the black prayer beads. 'I can even inform you that while I've been away you have breathed thirty-three times.' She crouches down. 'And even now, at this moment, as I'm speaking, I can count your breaths.' She lifts the string of prayer beads into what seems to be the man's field of vision. 'And now, since my return, you have breathed seven times.' She sits on the kilim and continues, 'I no longer count my days in hours, or my hours in minutes, or my minutes in seconds . . . a day for me is ninety-nine prayer-bead cycles!' Her gaze comes to rest on the old watch-bracelet holding together the bones of the man's wrist. 'I can even tell you that there are five cycles to go before

8

the Mullah makes the call to midday prayer and preaches the hadith.' A moment. She is working it out. 'At the twentieth cycle, the water bearer will knock on the neighbour's door. As usual, the old woman with the rasping cough will come out to open the door for him. At the thirtieth, a boy will cross the street on his bike, whistling the tune of '*Laïli, Laïli, Laïli, djân, djân, djân, you have broken my heart*', for our neighbour's daughter . . .' She laughs. A sad laugh. 'And when I reach the seventy-second cycle, that cretinous Mullah will come to visit you and, as always, will reproach me because, according to him, I can't have taken good care of you, can't have followed his instructions, must have neglected the prayers . . . Otherwise you'd be getting better!' She touches the man's arm. 'But you are my witness. You know that I live only for you, at your side, by your breath! It's easy for him to say,' she complains, 'that I must recite one of the ninety-nine names of God ninety-nine times a day . . . for ninety-nine days! But that stupid Mullah has no idea what it's like to be alone with a man who . . .' She can't find the right word, or doesn't dare say it, and just grumbles softly '. . . to be all alone with two little girls!'

A long silence. Almost five prayer-bead cycles. Five cycles during which the woman remains huddled against the wall, her eyes closed. It is the call to midday prayer that snatches her from her daze. She picks up the little rug, unfolds it and lays it out on the ground. Makes a start on the prayer.

The prayer complete, she remains sitting on the rug to listen to the Mullah preach the hadith for that day of the week: '. . . and today is a day of blood, for it was on a Tuesday that Eve, for the first time, lost tainted blood, that one of the sons of Adam killed his brother, that Gregory, Zachary and Yahya – may peace be upon them – were killed, as well as Pharaoh's counsellors, his wife Asiya Bint Muzahim, and the heifer of the Children of Israel . . .'

She looks around slowly. The room. Her man. This body in the emptiness. This empty body.

Her eyes fill with dread. She stands up, refolds the rug, puts it back in its place in the corner of the room, and leaves.

A few moments later, she returns to check the level of solution in the drip bag. There isn't much left.

She stares at the tube, noting the intervals between the drips. They are short, shorter than the intervals between the man's breaths. She adjusts the flow, waits two drips, and turns around decisively. 'I'm going to the pharmacy for more solution.' But before her feet cross the threshold, they falter and she lets out a plaintive sigh: 'I hope they've managed to get hold of some . . .' She leaves the room. We hear her waking the children, 'Come on, we're going out', and leaving, followed by little footsteps running down the passage, through the courtyard . . .

After three cycles of the prayer beads – two hundred and ninety-seven breaths – they are back.

The woman takes the children into the next-door room. One is crying, 'I'm hungry, Mummy.' The other complaining, 'Why didn't you get any bananas?' Their mother comforts them: 'I'll give you some bread.'

Just as the sun withdraws its rays from the holes in the yellow and blue sky of the curtains, the woman reappears in the doorway to the room. She looks at the man a while, then approaches and checks his breath. He is breathing. The drip bag is almost dry. 'The pharmacy was shut,' she says and, looking resigned, waits, as if for further instructions. Nothing. Nothing but breathing. She leaves again and returns with a glass of water. 'I'll have to do what I did last time, and use sugar-salt solution . . .'

With a quick, practised movement she pulls the tube out of his arm. Takes off the syringe. Cleans the tube, feeds it into his half-open mouth, and pushes it down until it reaches his oesophagus. Then she pours the contents of the glass into the drip bag. Adjusts the flow, checking the gaps between drips. One drip per breath.

And leaves.

A dozen drips later, she is back, chador in hand. 'I have to go and see my aunt.' She waits again . . . for permission, perhaps. Her eyes wander. 'I've lost my mind!' Agitated, she turns around and leaves the room. Behind the door her voice comes and goes in the passageway: 'I don't care', near, 'what you think of her . . .' far, 'I love her', near, 'she's all I have left . . . my sisters have abandoned me, and your brothers too . . .' far, '. . . that I see her', near, 'I need to . . .', far, '. . . she doesn't give a damn about you . . . and neither do I!' She can be heard leaving with her two children.

Their absence lasts three thousand nine hundred and sixty breaths. Three thousand nine hundred and sixty breaths during which nothing happens except what the woman had predicted. The water bearer knocks at the neighbour's door. A woman with a rasping cough opens the door to him . . . A few breaths later, a boy crosses the street on his bike whistling the tune of '*Laïli, Laïli, Laïli, djân, djân, djân, you have broken my heart . . .*'

So they return, she and her two children. She leaves them in the passage. Opens the door, abruptly. Her man is still there. Same position. Same rhythm to his breath. As for her, she is very pale. Paler even than him. She leans against the wall. After a long silence, she moans, 'My aunt . . . she has left the house . . . she's gone!' With her back to the wall she slips to the ground. 'She's gone . . . but where? No one knows . . . I have no one left . . . no one!' Her voice trembles. Her throat tightens. The tears flow. 'She doesn't know what's happened to me . . . she can't know! Otherwise she would have left me a message, or come to rescue me . . . She hates you, I know, but she loves me . . . she loves the children . . . but you . . .' The sobbing robs her of her voice. She moves away from the wall, shuts her eyes, takes a deep breath in an attempt to say something. But she can't say it; it must be heavy, heavy with meaning, voice-crushingly heavy. So she keeps it inside, and seeks something light, gentle, and easy to say: 'And you, you knew that you had a wife and two daughters!' She punches herself in the belly. Once. Twice. As if to beat out the heavy word that has buried itself in her guts. She crouches down and cries, 'Did you think about us for even a second, when you shouldered that fucking Kalashnikov? You son of a . . .', the words suppressed again.

She remains still for a moment. Her eyes close. Her head hangs. She lets out a long, painful groan. Her shoulders are still moving to the rhythm of the breath. Seven breaths.

Seven breaths, and she looks up, wiping her eyes on the sleeve embroidered with ears and flowers of corn. After looking at the man awhile, she moves closer, bends over his face and whispers, 'Forgive me', as she strokes his arm. 'I'm tired. At breaking point. Don't abandon me, you're all I have left.' She raises her voice: 'Without you, I have nothing. Think of your daughters! What will I do with them? They're so young . . .' She stops stroking him.

14

Somewhere outside, not far away, a shot is fired. Another, closer, in retort. The first gunman shoots again. This time, no response.

'The Mullah won't come today,' she says with some relief. 'He's scared of stray bullets. He's as much of a coward as your brothers.' She stands up and moves a few steps away. 'You men, you're all cowards!' She comes back. Stares darkly at the man. 'Where are your brothers who were so proud to see you fight their enemies?' Two breaths and her silence fills with rage. 'Cowards!' she spits. 'They should be looking after your children, and me – honouring you, and themselves – isn't that right? Where is your mother, who always used to say she would sacrifice herself for a single hair on your head? She couldn't deal with the fact that her son, the hero, who fought on every front, against every foe, had managed to get shot in a pathetic quarrel because some guy – from his own side, would you believe – had said, *I spit in your mother's pussy!* Shot over an insult!' She takes a step closer. 'It's so ridiculous, so stupid!' Her gaze wanders around the room and then settles, heavily, on the man who may or may not hear her. 'Do you know what your family said to me, before leaving the city?' she continues. 'That they wouldn't be able to take care of either your wife or your children . . . You might as well know: they've abandoned you. They don't give a fuck about your health, or your suffering, or your honour! . . . They've deserted us,' she cries. 'Us, me!' She raises her prayer-bead hand to the ceiling, begging, 'Allah, help me! . . . *Al-Qahhar, Al-Qahhar . . .*' And weeps.

One cycle of the prayer beads.

Desolate, she stammers, 'I'm going . . . I'm going . . . I am . . . mad.' She throws her head back. 'Why tell him all this? I'm going mad. Allah, cut off my tongue! May my mouth be filled with earth!' She covers her face. 'Allah, protect me, guide me, I'm losing my way, show me the path!'

No reply.

No guide.

Her hand buries itself in her man's hair. Beseeching words emerge from her dry throat: 'Come back, I beg you, before I lose my mind. Come back, for the sake of your children . . .' She looks up. Gazes through her tears in the same uncertain direction as the man. 'Bring him back to life, God!' Her voice drops. 'After all, he fought in your name for so long. For Jihad!' She stops, then starts

16

again: 'And you're leaving him in this state? What about his children? And me? You can't, you can't, you've no right to leave us like this, without a man!' Her left hand, the one holding the prayer beads, pulls the Koran towards her. Her rage seeks expression in her voice. 'Prove that you exist, bring him back to life!' She opens the Koran. Her finger moves down the names of God featured on the flyleaf. 'I swear I won't ever let him go off to fight again like a bloody idiot. Not even in your name! He will be mine, here, with me.' Her throat, knotted by sobs, lets through only the stifled cry '*Al-Qahhar.*' She starts telling the prayer beads again '*Al-Qahhar . . .*' Ninety-nine times, '*Al-Qahhar*'.

The room grows dark.

'I'm scared, Mummy. It's all dark.' One of the little girls is whimpering in the passage, behind the door. The woman stands up to leave the room.

'Don't be frightened, darling. I'm here.'

'Why are you shouting? You're scaring me, Mummy,' weeps the little girl. The mother reassures her: 'I wasn't shouting. I was talking to your father.'

They walk away from the door.

'Why are you calling my father *Al-Qahhar*? Is he cross?'

'No, but he will be if we disturb him.'

The little girl falls silent.

It is now completely dark.

And, as the woman predicted, the Mullah has not come.

She returns with a hurricane lamp. Puts it on the ground near the man's head, and takes the bottle of eye drops out of her pocket. Gently, she administers the drops. One, two. One, two. Then leaves the room and comes back with a sheet and a small plastic basin. She removes the dirty sheet covering the man's legs. Washes his belly, his feet, his genitals. Once this is done she covers her man with a clean sheet, checks the gaps between the drips of sugar-salt solution and leaves, taking the lamp with her.

Everything is dark once more. For a long time.

At dawn, as the hoarse voice of the Mullah calls the faithful to prayer, the sound of dragging feet can be heard in the passage. They approach the room, move away, then come back. The door opens. The woman enters. She looks at the man. Her man. He is still there, in the same position. But his eyes draw her attention. She takes a step forward. His eyes are closed. The woman moves nearer. Another step. Silently. Then two. She looks at him. Can't see clearly. She isn't sure. She backs out of the room. Less than five breaths later she is back with the hurricane lamp. His eyes are still closed. She collapses on to the floor. 'Are you sleeping?!' Her trembling hand moves to the man's chest. He is breathing. 'Yes . . . you're sleeping!' she shouts. Looks around the room for someone so she can say it again: 'He's sleeping!'

No one. She is afraid.

She picks up the little rug, unfolds it and stretches it out on the ground. The morning prayer done, she remains sitting, takes the Koran and opens it at the page marked with a peacock feather, which she removes and holds in her right hand. With her left, she tells the prayer beads.

After reading a few verses, she puts back the feather, closes the Koran, and sits thoughtfully for a moment, gazing at the feather peeking out of the sacred book. She strokes it, sadly at first, then anxiously.

She stands up, tidies away the rug and walks towards the door. Before leaving, she stops. Turns around.

Goes back to her place by the man. Hesitantly opens one of his eyes. Then the other. Waits. His eyes do not close again. The woman takes the bottle of eye drops and measures a few drops into his eyes. One, two. One, two. Checks the drip bag. There's still some solution.

Before standing up, she pauses and looks nervously at the man, asking him, 'Can you close your eyes again?' The man's vacant eyes do not respond. She persists, 'You can, you can! Do it again!' And waits. In vain.

Concerned, she slips her hand gently under the man's neck. A sensation, a horror, makes her arm twitch. She shuts her eyes, clenches her teeth. Breathes in deeply, painfully. She is suffering. As she breathes out, she extracts her hand and examines the tips of her trembling fingers in the weak light of the lamp. They are dry. She stands up to roll the man on to his side. Brings the lamp closer to his neck so she can examine a small wound – still open, bruised, drained of blood but not yet healed.

The woman holds her breath, and presses the wound. The man still doesn't respond. She presses harder. No protest. Not in the eyes, or the breath. 'Doesn't it even hurt?' She rolls the man on to his back again, and leans over him so she can look into his eyes. 'You don't suffer! You've never suffered, never! I've never heard of a man surviving a bullet in the neck! You're not even bleeding, there's no pus, no pain, no suffering! "*It's a miracle!*" your mother used to say . . . Some bloody miracle!' She stands up. 'Even injured, you've been spared suffering.' Her voice rasps in her tightening throat. 'And it's me who suffers! Me who cries!' Having said it, she moves to the door. Tears and fury in her eyes, she disappears into the darkness of the passage, leaving the hurricane lamp to project the trembling shadow of the man on to the wall until the full rise of dawn, until the rays of the sun make their way through the holes in the yellow and blue curtains, condemning the lamp to insignificance.

A hand hesitates to open the door to the room. Or is struggling to. 'Daddy!' The voice of one of the children can be heard over the creaking of the door. 'Where are you going?' At the woman's shout, the child pulls the door shut and moves away. 'Don't bother your father, darling. He's sick. He's sleeping. Come with me!' The small footsteps run off down the passage. 'But what about you, when you go in there, and shout, doesn't that bother him?' Her mother replies: 'Yes, it does.' Silence.

A fly sneaks into the heavy hush of the room. Lands on the man's forehead. Hesitant. Uncertain. Wanders over his wrinkles, licks his skin. No taste. Definitely no taste.

The fly makes its way down into the corner of his eye. Still hesitant. Still uncertain. It tastes the white of the eye, then moves off. Nothing chases it away. It resumes its journey, getting lost in the beard, climbing the nose. Takes flight. Explores the body. Returns. Settles once more on the face. Clambers on to the tube stuffed into the half-open mouth. Licks it, moves right along it to the edge of the lips. No spit. No taste. The fly continues, enters the mouth. And is engulfed.

The hurricane lamp breathes its final breaths in vain. The flame goes out. The woman returns. She is filled with a deep weariness – of her being, and her body. After a few listless steps towards her man, she stops. Less decisive than the previous day. Her gaze lingers desperately on the motionless body. She sits down between the man and the Koran, which she opens at the flyleaf. She moves her finger over the names of God, one by one. Counts them. Stops at the seventeenth name. Murmurs '*Al-Wahhab, the Bestower*'. A bitter smile puckers the edges of her lips. 'I don't need a gift.' She pulls at the peacock feather peeking out of the Koran. 'I haven't the heart to go on reciting the names of God.' She strokes her lips with the feather. 'Praise be to God . . . He will save you. Without me. Without my prayers . . . he's got to.'

The woman is silenced by a knocking at the door. 'It must be the Mullah.' She hasn't the slightest desire to open. More knocking. She hesitates. The knocking continues. She leaves the room. Her footsteps can be heard moving towards the road. She is talking to someone. Her words are lost in the courtyard, behind the windows.

A hand timidly pushes open the door to the room. One of the little girls comes in. A sweet face beneath a mop of unruly hair. She is slender. Her little eyes stare at the man. 'Daddy!' she cries, and shyly walks closer. 'Are you sleeping, Daddy?' she asks. 'What's that in your mouth?' pointing at the drip tube. She stops near her father, unsure whether to touch his cheek. 'But you're not sleeping!' she cries. 'Why does Mummy always say you're sleeping? Mummy says you're sick. She won't let me come in here and talk to you . . . but she's always talking to you.' She is about to sit down next to him when she is stopped by a cry from her sister, squeezed into the half-open doorway. 'Be quiet!' she shouts, mimicking her mother's voice, and runs up to the little one. 'Come on!' She takes her by the hand and pulls her towards their father. After a moment's hesitation, the younger girl climbs on to her father's chest and starts yanking at his beard. The other shouts heartily, 'Come on, Daddy, talk!' She leans towards his mouth and touches the tube. 'Take out this thing. Talk!' She pulls away the tube, hoping to hear him say something. But no. Nothing but breathing. Slow, deep breaths. She stares at her father's half-open mouth. Her curious little hand dives in and pulls out the fly. 'A fly!' she cries and, disgusted, throws it on the floor. The younger girl laughs, and rests her chapped cheek on her father's chest.

The mother comes in. 'What are you doing?' she screams in horror. She rushes towards the children, grabbing them by the arms. 'Get out! Come with me!'

'A fly! Daddy's eating a fly!' shriek the girls, almost in concert. 'Be quiet!' orders their mother.

They leave the room.

The fly struggles on the kilim, drowning in saliva.

The woman comes back into the room. Before rein-
serting the tube into the man's mouth she looks
around, anxious and intrigued. 'What fly?' Noticing
nothing, she replaces the tube and leaves.

Later, she comes back to pour sugar-salt solution
into the drip bag, and eye drops into the man's eyes.

Her tasks complete, she does not remain with her
man.

She no longer puts her right hand on her man's
chest.

She no longer tells the black prayer beads in time
with her man's breathing.

She leaves.

She doesn't return until the call to midday prayer
– and not to take out the little carpet, unfurl it, lay
it on the ground and say her prayers. Just to put
new eye drops into the man's eyes. One, two. One,
two. And then leave again.

After the call to prayer, the Mullah's hoarse voice
beseeches God to lend his protection to the area's
faithful on this, a Wednesday: '. . . because, as our
Prophet says, *it's a day of misfortune during which*

the Pharaoh and his people were drowned, and the peoples of the Prophet Salih – the Ad and the Thamoud – were destroyed . . .' He stops and immediately starts again in a fearful voice. 'Dear Faithful, as I have always told you, Wednesday is a day on which, according to our Prophet, the most noble, *it is right neither to practise bloodletting, nor to give, nor to receive.* However, one of the hadith, quoted by Ibn Younes, says that this practice is permitted during Jihad. Today, your brother, our great Commander, is furnishing you with weapons that you may defend your honour, your blood, and your tribe!'

In the street, men are shouting themselves hoarse: '*Allah O Akbar!*' Running: '*Allah O Akbar!*' Their voices fading as they near the mosque: '*Allah O . . .*'

A few ants prowl around the corpse of the fly on the kilim. Then grab hold of it and carry it off.

The woman arrives to gaze anxiously at the man. Perhaps she is afraid that the call to arms will have put him back on his feet.

She stays near the door. Her fingers stroke her lips and then, nervously, stray between her teeth, as if to extract words that don't dare express themselves. She leaves the room. She can be heard making something for lunch, talking and playing with the children.

Then it's time for a nap.

Darkness.

Silence.

The woman comes back. Less anxious. She sits down next to the man. 'That was the Mullah. He was here for our prayer session. I told him that since yesterday I have been impure, that I am menstruating, like Eve. He wasn't happy. I'm not sure why. Because I dared compare myself to Eve, or because I told him I was bleeding? He left, muttering into his beard. He wasn't like that before; you could have a joke with him. But since you people declared this new law for the country, he's changed too. He's afraid, poor man.'

Her gaze settles on the Koran. Suddenly, she jumps: 'Shit, the feather!' She looks for it inside the book. Not there. Under the pillow. Not there either. In her pockets. There it is. With a big sigh, she sits down. 'That Mullah is driving me out of my mind!' she says as she puts the feather back inside the Koran. 'What was I talking about? . . .

Oh yes, bleeding . . . I was lying to him, of course.' She glances keenly at the man, more mischievous than submissive. 'Just as I've lied to you . . . more than once!' She pulls her legs up to her chest and wedges her chin between her knees. 'But there is something I'd better tell you . . .' She looks at him for a long time. Still with the same strange wariness in her gaze. 'You know . . .' Her voice goes hoarse. She swallows to moisten her throat, and looks up. 'When you and I went to bed for the first time – after three years of marriage, remember! – anyway, that night, I had my period.' Her gaze flees the man to seek refuge in the creases of the sheet. She rests her left cheek on her knees. The look in her scarred eye loses some of its wariness. 'I didn't tell you. And you, you thought that . . . the blood was proof of my virginity!' A muted laugh shakes her crouched, huddled body. 'How thrilled you were to see the blood, how proud!' A moment. A look. And the dread of hearing a cry of rage, an insult. Nothing. And so, soft and serene, she allows herself to visit the intimate corners of her memory. 'I shouldn't really have had my period then. It wasn't the right time, but I was a week early; it must have been nerves, fear about meeting you. I mean, can you imagine – being engaged for almost a year and then married for three years to an absent man; not so easy. I lived with your name. I had never seen or heard or touched you before that day. I was afraid, afraid of everything, of you, of going to bed, of the blood. But at the same time, it was a fear I enjoyed. You know, the kind of fear that doesn't separate you from your desire, but instead arouses you, gives you wings, even though it may burn. That was the kind of fear I was feeling. And it was growing in me every day, invading my belly, my guts . . . On the night before you arrived, it came pouring out. It wasn't a blue fear. No. It was a red fear, blood red. When I mentioned it to my aunt she advised me not to say anything . . . and so I kept quiet. That suited me fine. Although I was a virgin I was really scared. I kept wondering what would happen if by any chance I didn't bleed that night . . .' Her hand sweeps through the air as if batting away a fly. 'It would have been a catastrophe. I'd heard so many stories about that. I could imagine the whole thing.' Her voice becomes mocking. 'Passing off impure blood as virginal blood, bit of a brainwave, don't you think?' She lies down right close to the man. 'I have never understood why, for you men, pride is so much linked to blood.' Her hand sweeps the air again. Her fingers are moving. As if gesturing to an invisible person to come closer. 'And remember the night – it was when we were first living together – that you came home late. Dead drunk. You'd been smoking. I had fallen asleep. You pulled down my knickers without saying a word. I woke up. But I pretended to be deeply asleep. You . . . penetrated me . . . you had a great time . . . but when you stood up to go and wash yourself, you noticed blood on your dick. You were furious. You came back and beat me, in the middle of the night, just because I hadn't warned you that I was bleeding. I had defiled you!' She laughs, scornful. 'I had made you unclean.' Her hand snatches memories from the air, closes around them, descends to stroke her belly as it swells and slackens at a pace faster than the man's breathing.

Suddenly, she thrusts her hand downwards, beneath her dress, between her legs. Closes her eyes. Takes a deep, ragged breath. Rams her fingers into herself, roughly, as if driving in a blade. Holding her breath, she pulls out her hand with a stifled cry. Opens her eyes and looks at the tips of her nails. They are wet. Wet with blood. Red with blood. She puts her hand in front of the man's vacant eyes. 'Look! That's my blood, too. Clean. What's the difference between menstrual blood and blood that is clean? What's so disgusting about this blood?' Her hand moves down to the man's nostrils. 'You were born of this blood! It is cleaner than the blood of your own body!' She pushes her fingers roughly into his beard. As she brushes his lips she feels his breath. A shiver of fear runs across her skin. Her arm shudders. She pulls her hand away, clenches her fist and, with her mouth against the pillow, cries out again. Just once. The cry is long. Heartrending. She doesn't move for a long time. A very long time. Until the water bearer knocks on the neighbour's door, and the old woman's rasping cough is heard through the walls, and the water bearer empties his skin into the neighbour's tank, and one of her daughters starts crying in the passage. Then, she stands up and leaves the room without daring to look at her man.

Later, much later, just as the ants carrying the fly's body reach the foot of the wall between the two windows, the woman comes back with a clean sheet and the small plastic basin. She pulls off the sheet covering the man's legs, washes his belly, feet and penis

. . . and covers him up again. 'More repugnant than a corpse! He doesn't give off any smell at all!' She leaves.

Night, again.

The room in absolute darkness.

Suddenly, the blinding flash of an explosion. A deafening blast makes the earth tremble. Its breath shatters the windows.

Throats are torn apart by screaming.

A second explosion. This one closer. Therefore more violent.

The children are crying.

The woman is wailing.

The sound of their terrified footsteps rings out in the passage, and disappears into the cellar.

Outside, not far away, something catches fire – perhaps the neighbour's tree. The light rips through the dusk of the courtyard and the room.

Outside, some are yelling, some crying, and some firing their Kalashnikovs, who knows where from or towards whom . . . just firing, firing . . .

It all stops eventually, in the grey half-light of an undecided dawn.

Then a thick silence descends on the smoky street,

on the courtyard now nothing but a dead garden, on the room where the man, covered in soot, is laid out as always. Motionless. Immune. Just breathing. Slowly breathing.

The hesitant creaking of an opening door and the sound of cautious footsteps proceeding along the passage do not shatter this deathly silence, but underline it.

The footsteps stop behind the door. After a long pause – four of the man's breaths – the door opens. It's the woman. She enters. Does not look at him straight away. First, she examines the state of the room, the broken window panes, the soot now settled on the curtains' migrating birds, on the kilim's faded stripes, on the open Koran, on the drip bag emptying itself of its last salty-sweet drops . . . Then her gaze sweeps over the sheet covering the man's skeletal legs, takes in his beard and finally reaches his eyes.

She takes a few fearful steps towards the man. Stops. Observes the movement of his chest. He is breathing. She walks closer, bends down so she can see his eyes more clearly. They are open, and covered in black dust. She wipes them with the end of her sleeve, takes out the bottle and administers drops to each eye. One, two. One, two.

She touches the man's face cautiously, to wipe off the soot, and then sits quite still, as still as him. Her shoulders weighed down with troubles, she breathes, as always, to the same rhythm as the man.

The neighbour's rasping cough travels through the silence of the grey dawn, turning the woman's head towards the yellow and blue sky of the curtains. She stands up and goes to the window, crushing shards of glass beneath her feet. She looks for the neighbour through the holes in the curtains. A shrill cry bursts from her chest. She rushes to the door, and out into the passage. But the deafening sound of a tank freezes her in her tracks. Bewildered, she comes back. 'The door . . . our door on to the street has been destroyed. The neighbour's walls . . .' Her horrified voice is muffled by the roar of the tank. Her gaze travels once more around the room, stopping sharply at the window. She walks up to it, parts the curtains and gasps. 'Not that! No, not that!'

The noise of the tank starts to fade; the neighbour's coughing is heard again.

The woman collapses on the shards of glass. Eyes closed, voice muffled, she begs, 'God . . . merciful God, I belong to . . .' A shot rings out. She is silent. A second shot. Then a man's cry:

'*Allah O Akbar!*' The tank fires. The explosion shakes the house, and the woman. She hurls herself to the ground, slithers to the door, makes it into the passage, and hurtles down the cellar stairs to her terrified daughters.

The man remains motionless. Impassive.

When the shots cease – a lack of ammunition, perhaps – the tank drives away. The thick, smoky silence returns and settles.

In this dusty stillness, at the foot of the wall between the two windows, a spider is prowling around the carcass of the fly discarded by the ants. Examining it. Then it too abandons the fly, takes a tour of the room, returns to the window, attaches itself to the curtain, climbs it, and crawls over the migrating birds frozen in the yellow and blue sky. It leaves the sky and climbs on to the ceiling, to disappear among the rotting beams, where it will spin its web, no doubt.

The woman reappears. Once again carrying the plastic basin, a towel and a sheet. She cleans up. The shards of glass, the soot that has spread all over the room, everything. Then she leaves. Comes back. Pours sugar-salt solution into the drip bag, returns to her spot at the man's side, and administers the bottle's remaining eye drops. One. She waits. Two. She stops. The bottle is empty. She leaves.

On the ceiling, the spider reappears. Hanging from the end of its silken thread, it moves slowly downwards. Lands on the man's chest. After a few moments' hesitation it follows the sinuous lines of the sheet up towards his beard. Suspicious, it turns away and slips between the folds of fabric.

The woman returns. 'There is going to be more fighting!' she announces, and walks purposefully towards the man. 'I'm going to have to take you down into the cellar.' She pulls the tube out of his mouth, and wedges her hands under his armpits. Lifts him. Drags his scrawny body. Pulls him on to the kilim. Then stops. 'I'm not strong enough . . .' She is desperate. 'I'll never manage to get you down the stairs.'

She drags him back on to the mattress. Reinserts the tube. Stands there for a moment, not moving. Upset and out of breath, she stares down at him. 'It would be better if a stray bullet just finished you off, once and for all!' she says finally. She stands up abruptly to draw the curtains, and storms out of the room.

The neighbour's cough can be heard, ripping through the afternoon silence in the same way it racks her chest. She must be walking on the ruins of her home. Her slow, faltering steps wander through the garden, move closer to the house. Here is her broken shadow on the curtains' migrating birds. She coughs and murmurs an inaudible name. She coughs. She waits. In vain. She moves off, murmurs the name again, and coughs. No response. She calls, she coughs. She is no longer waiting. No longer murmuring. She is humming something. Names, perhaps. Then she walks away. Far away. And returns. Her hum can still be heard, over the sound of the street. Over the sound of boots. The boots of men carrying weapons. The boots are running. Scattering. In order to hide somewhere presumably – behind the walls, in the rubble . . . and wait for the night.

The water bearer doesn't come today. The boy doesn't cross the road on his bicycle whistling the tune of '*Laïli, Laïli, Laïli, djân, djân, djân, you have broken my heart . . .*'

Everyone is lying low. They are silent. Waiting.

Now night falls on the city, and the city falls into the drowsiness of fear.

But nobody shoots.

The woman comes into the room to check on the sugar-salt solution in the drip bag, and leaves again. Without a word.

The old neighbour is still coughing, still humming to herself. She is neither near nor far. She must be among the ruins of the wall that, so recently, separated the two houses.

A heavy, ominous sleep steals over the house, over all the houses, over the whole street, with the old neighbour's hummed lament in the background, a lament that continues until she hears noise again, the noise of boots. She stops humming, but continues coughing. 'They're coming back!' Her voice trembles in the vast blackness of the night.

The boots are near, now. Arriving. They chase away the old lady, enter the courtyard of the house, and keep coming. They come right up to the window. The barrel of a gun pokes through one of the shattered panes, pushing aside the curtains patterned with migrating birds. The butt breaks open the whole window. Three yelling men hurl themselves into the room. 'Nobody move!' And nothing does move. One of them switches on a torch and points it at the motionless man, barking, 'Stay where you are, or I'll smash your head in!' He puts a booted foot on the man's chest. The faces and the heads of the three men are hidden by black turbans. They surround the man, who continues to breathe slowly and silently. One of the three bends over him. 'Shit, he's got a tube in his mouth!' He pulls it out and yells, 'Where's your weapon?' The recumbent man continues to stare blankly at the ceiling, his gaze lost in the darkness where the spider may already have spun its web. 'We're talking to you!' screams the man holding the torch. 'He's fucked!' concludes the second man, crouching down to pull off the watch and the gold wedding ring. The third man rifles through the whole room – under the mattress and pillows, behind the plain green curtain, under the kilim . . . 'There's nothing here!' he complains. 'Go and check the other rooms!' orders the other, the first man, the one with the torch in his hand and his boot on the man's chest. The other two obey. They disappear into the passage.

The one who is left lifts the sheet with the barrel of his gun, exposing the man's body. Perturbed by its lifelessness, its total silence, he grinds the heel of his boot into the man's chest. 'What d'you think you're looking at?' He waits for a groan. Nothing. No protest. Flustered, he tries again. 'Do you hear me?' He scans the vacant face. Exasperated, he scolds, 'Cut your tongue out, did they?', then snorts, 'Already dead, are you?' Finally, he falls silent.

After a deep, angry breath, he grabs the man by the collar and lifts him up. The man's pale and disturbing face scares him. He lets go and backs away, stopping in the doorway, unsettled. 'Where are you, boys?' he grumbles from behind the strip of turban muffling his voice. He glances into the passage, dark as blackest night, and shouts, 'Are you there?' His voice rings out in the emptiness. Like the man's, his breathing becomes slow and deep. He walks back over to the man, to stare at him again. Something intrigues him, and distresses him. His torch sweeps over the motionless body, returning once more to the wide open eyes. He kicks him gently on the shoulder with the tip of his boot. Still no reaction. Nothing. He swings his weapon into the man's field of vision, then rests the barrel on his forehead and presses down. Nothing. Still nothing. He takes another deep breath, and goes back to the doorway. At last, he hears the others sniggering in one of the rooms. 'What the fuck are they doing?' he grumbles, afraid. His two comrades come back laughing.

'What did you find?'

'Look!' says one of them, brandishing a bra. 'He's got a wife!'

'Yes, I know.'

'You know?'

'You moron, you took off his wedding ring, didn't you?'

The second man drops the bra on the floor, joking with his mate: 'She must have tiny tits!' But the man with the torch doesn't laugh. He is thinking. 'I'm sure I know him,' he mutters as he approaches the man. The other two follow.

'Who is it?'

'I don't know his name.'

'Is he one of ours?'

'I think so.'

They remain standing, faces still hidden behind the strips of black turban.

'Did he speak?'

'No, he doesn't say a word. He doesn't move.'

One of the men kicks him.

'Hey, wake up!'

'Stop that, can't you see his eyes are already open?'

'Did you finish him off?'

The man holding the torch shakes his head, and asks, 'Where is his wife?'

'There's no one in the house.'

Silence, again. A long silence in which everything is pulled into sync with the man's breathing. Slow and heavy. At last one of the men cracks. 'What shall we do then? Get out of here?' No response.

They don't move.

The old neighbour's chant is heard again, interspersed with her rasping cough. 'The madwoman's back,' says one man. 'Perhaps it's his mother,' suggests the other. The third leaves the room via the window, and rushes up to the old woman. 'Do you live here, Mother?' She hums, 'I live here . . .' She coughs. 'I live there . . .' She coughs. 'I live wherever I like, with my daughter, with the king, wherever I like . . . with my daughter, with the king . . .' She coughs. Again the man chases her away from the rubble of her own house, and returns. 'She's gone completely nuts!'

The coughing retreats and is lost in the distance.

The man with the torch notices the Koran on the ground, rushes up to it, grabs it, prostrates himself, and kisses the book as he prays behind the strip of his turban. 'He's a good Muslim!' he cries.

They plunge back into their silent thoughts. Remain there, until one – the same one – becomes impatient. 'Right, what the fuck are we doing? Let's patrol! Shit! We didn't bomb the area for nothing, right?'

They stand up.

The one holding the torch covers the man's body with the sheet, puts the tube back in his mouth, and gestures to the other two to leave.

Off they go. With the Koran.

Dawn, again.

The woman's footsteps, again.

She climbs the stairs from the cellar, walks down the passage and enters the room, not noticing that the door is open and the curtains too; not suspecting for a moment that visitors have forced their way in.

She glances at her man. He is breathing. She leaves and comes back with two glasses of water. One for the drip bag, the other to moisten the man's eyes. Even now, she notices nothing. It must be because of the shadowy light. Day has not yet broken, the sun has not yet shone through the hole-studded sky of the curtains patterned with migrating birds. It is only later, when she comes back to change the man's sheet and shirt, that she finally notices his bare wrist and finger. 'Where's your watch? Your ring?' She checks his hands, his pockets. She rummages around under the sheet. Unsettled, she takes a few steps towards the door, then comes back. 'What's going on?' She is worried, then panicked. 'Did someone come?' she asks herself, going to the window. 'Yes, someone did come!' she exclaims, terrorised, as she sees how it has been smashed. 'And yet . . . I didn't hear anything!' She backs away. 'I was sleeping! My God, how can I have slept so deeply?' Horrified, she runs to the passage, leaving the man uncovered. Comes back. Picks up her bra from the doorway. 'Did they search the house? But they didn't come down to the cellar?' She collapses next to the man, grabs his arm and cries, 'It was you . . . you moved! You're doing all this to terrify me! To drive me mad! It's you!' She shakes him roughly. Pulls out the tube.

Waits. Still no sign, no sound. Her head hunches into her shoulders. A sob tears through her chest, shaking her whole body. After a long burdened sigh, she stands up, wipes her eyes on the end of her sleeve and, before leaving, reinserts the tube into the man's mouth.

She can be heard inspecting the other rooms. She stops when the neighbour's rasping cough comes near the house. She rushes into the courtyard and calls out to the old woman, '*Bibi* . . . Did someone come here last night?'

'Yes, my daughter, the king came . . .' She coughs. 'He came to visit me . . . he caressed me . . .' She laughs, coughing. 'Do you have any bread, daughter? I gave all mine to the king . . . he was hungry. How handsome he was! To die for! He asked me to sing.' She starts singing. '*Oh, king of goodness / I weep in loneliness / Oh, king . . .*'

'Where are the others?' the woman asks. 'Your husband, your son?' The old lady stops singing and continues her tale in a sad voice. 'The king wept, as he listened to me! He even asked my husband and son to dance to my song. They danced. The king asked them to dance the dance of the dead . . . They didn't know it . . .' She smiles, before continuing:

'So he taught them, by cutting off their heads and pouring boiling oil on their bodies . . . Well that made them dance!' She takes up her lament once more. '*Oh king, know that my heart can no longer bear your absence / It is time for you to come back . . .*' The woman stops her again. 'But what . . . my God . . . your house! Your husband, your son . . . are they alive?' The old lady's voice becomes shrill, like a child's. 'Yes, they are here, my husband and son are here, in the house . . .' She coughs. 'With their heads under their arms.' She coughs. 'Because they are angry with me'. The old woman coughs, and weeps. 'They won't talk to me any more! Because I gave the king all our bread. Do you want to see them?'

'But . . .'

'Come on! Talk to them!'

The women walk off across the rubble. They can no longer be heard.

Suddenly, a howl. From the woman. Horrified. Horrifying. Her footsteps stagger over the flag-stones, stumble through the ruins, cross the garden and enter the house. She is still screaming. She vomits. Weeps. Runs around the house. Like a madwoman. 'I'm leaving this place. I'm going to find my aunt. Whatever the cost!' Her panicky voice fills the passage, the rooms, the cellar. Then she comes back up, with her children. They flee the house without stopping to check on the man. The sound of them leaving is accompanied by the old woman's coughing and chanting, which makes the children laugh.

Everything is absorbed into the man's silence and passivity.

And this continues.

For a long time.

Once in a while, flies' wings sweep through the silence. At first their flight is decisive, but after a tour of the room they become engrossed in the man's body. Then leave again.

Occasionally, a gust of wind lifts the curtains. It plays with the migrating birds frozen on the yellow and blue sky studded with holes.

Even a wasp, with its ominous buzzing, is not able to disturb the torpor of the room. It circles the man again and again, lands on his forehead – stings him or not, we shall never know – and flies off towards the ceiling, presumably to build itself a nest amid the rotting beams. Its dreams of nesting come to an abrupt end in the spider's trap.

It wriggles. And then nothing.

Nothing then.

Night falls.

Shots ring out.

The neighbour returns, with her singing and her lugubrious cough. And immediately goes off again.

The woman does not come back.

Dawn.

The Mullah performs his call to prayer.

The weapons are asleep. But the smoke and smell of gunpowder maintain their presence.

It's when the first rays of sunlight pierce the holes in the yellow and blue sky of the curtains that the woman returns. Alone. She walks straight into the room, straight to her man. First she takes off her veil. Stands there a moment. Looking around, checking everything. Nothing has been moved. Nothing has been taken. The drip bag is empty, that's all.

Reassured, the woman comes to life. She walks unsteadily to the mattress on which the man is lying, half naked, as she left him the previous night. Stares at him a long time, as if again counting his breaths. She starts to sit down but suddenly freezes, crying 'The Koran!' Once more her eyes fill with dread. She searches every inch of the room. No sign of the word of God. 'The prayer beads?' She finds them under the pillow. 'Has someone been here again?' Again the doubt. Again the fear. 'The Koran was here yesterday, wasn't it?' Unsure, she sinks to the floor. Then suddenly cries, 'The feather!' and starts scrabbling around in a frenzy. 'My God! The feather!'

From outside comes the sound of children's voices. Local kids, playing in the rubble.

'*Hajii mor'alé?*'

'*Balé?*'

'Who wants water? Who wants fire?'

The woman goes over to the window, parts the curtains and calls to the children: 'Did you see anyone come into this house?' 'No!' they all shout at once, and carry on with their game: 'I want fire!'

She leaves the room, inspects the whole house.

Wearily she comes back and leans against the wall between the two windows. 'But who is coming here? What do they do to you?' Worry and distress

49

are visible in her eyes. 'We can't stay here!' She falls silent suddenly, as if interrupted. Then, after a brief hesitation, continues: 'But what can I do with you? Where can I take you in this state? I think . . .' Her gaze falls on the empty drip bag. 'I've got to get water,' she says to give herself time. She stands up, goes out, comes back with the two glasses of water. Carries out her daily tasks. Sits down. Keeping vigil. Thinking. Which allows her, after a few breaths, to announce almost triumphantly, 'I've managed to find my aunt. She's moved to the northern part of the city, to a safer area, to her cousin's house.' A pause. The habitual pause, waiting for a reaction that doesn't come. So she continues: 'I left the children with her.' Again, she pauses. Then, over-whelmed, mutters, 'I'm afraid, here', as if to justify her decision. Receiving no reaction at all, no word of agreement, she looks down as she lowers her voice. 'I'm afraid of you!' She searches the floor for something. Words. But more importantly, courage. She finds them, grabs them, and hurls them at him: 'I can't do anything for you. I think it's all over!' She falls silent again, then talks quickly, firmly. 'It seems this neighbourhood is going to be the next front line between the factions.' She adds, furiously, 'You knew, didn't you?' Another pause, just a breath to gather the strength to say, 'Your brothers knew, too. That's why they all left. They've abandoned us! The cowards! They didn't take me with them because you were alive. If . . .' She swallows her spit, and her rage as well. Continues, less fiercely, 'If . . . if you had died, things would have been different . . .' She interrupts that thought. Hesitates. After a deep breath, decides: 'One of them would have had to marry me!' Her voice shakes with a silent snigger. 'Perhaps they would have been happier if you had died.' She shudders. 'That way, they could have . . . fucked me! With a clear conscience.' Having said it, she stands up suddenly and leaves the room. Paces nervously up and down the passage. Searching for something. Calm. Serenity. But returns more febrile still. She rushes at the man and gabbles it all out in a rush: 'Your brothers have always wanted to fuck me! They . . .' Walks away, and back again. 'They spied on me . . . constantly, for the whole three years you were away . . . spied on me through the little window in the bath house while I was washing myself . . . and . . . jerked off. They spied on us too, at night . . .' Her lips tremble. Her hands move feverishly through the air, through her hair, through the folds of her dress. Her footsteps stumble on the faded stripes of the old kilim. 'They jerk . . .'

She breaks off, and again storms furiously out of the room, for a breath of fresh air and to purge herself of her rage. 'The fuckers!' she yells in exasperation. 'The bastards!' And can immediately be heard weeping and begging: 'What am I saying? Why am I saying all this? Help me, God! I can't control myself. I don't know what I'm saying . . .'

She walls herself up in silence.

The children who were playing in the rubble can no longer be seen either. They have moved off at last.

The woman reappears. Her hair in a mess. A wild look in her eyes. After a little walk around, she sinks down by the man's head. 'I don't know what's happening to me. My strength is deserting me, day by day. Just like my faith. I need you to understand.' She strokes him. 'I hope you are able to think, to hear, to see . . . to see me, and hear me . . .' She leans against the wall, and lets a long moment go by – a dozen cycles of the prayer beads, perhaps, as if she were still telling them to the rhythm of the man's breathing – enough time to think, to explore the nooks and crannies of her life, and return with memories. 'You never listened to me, never heard me! We never spoke about any of this! We've been married for more than ten years, but only lived together for two or three. Isn't that right?' She counts. 'Yes, ten and a half years of marriage, three years of conjugal life! It's only now that I'm counting. Only now that I'm realising all this!' A smile. A short, false smile worth a thousand words of regret and remorse . . . but very soon, the memories take hold. 'At the time, I didn't even question your absence. It seemed so normal! You were at the front. You were fighting for freedom, for Allah! And that made everything okay. It gave me hope, made me proud. In some way, you were with us. Inside each of us.' She is looking back, seeing it all again . . . 'Your mother, with her enormous bust, coming to our place to ask for the hand of my younger sister. It wasn't her turn to get married. It was my turn. So your mother simply said, "*No problem, we'll take her instead!*", pointing her fleshy finger at me as I poured the tea. I panicked and knocked the pot over.' She hides her face in her hands. In shame, or to dispel the image of a mocking mother-in-law. 'As for you, you didn't even know this was happening. My father, who wanted nothing more, accepted without the slightest hesitation. He didn't give a damn that you weren't around! Who were you, really? No one knew. To all of us, you were just a title: the Hero! And, like every hero, far away. Engagement to a hero was a lovely thing, for a seventeen-year-old girl. I said to myself, "God is far away, too, and yet I love him, and believe in him . . ."Anyway, they celebrated our engagement without the fiancé. Your mother said, "*Don't worry, victory is coming! It will soon be the end of the war, we will be free, and my son will return!*" Nearly a year later, your mother came back. Victory was still a long way off. "*It's dangerous to leave a young, engaged woman with her parents for such a long time!*" she said. And so I had to be married, despite your absence. At the ceremony, you were present in the form of a photo, and that wretched khanjar, which they put next to me in place of you. And I had to wait another three years for you. Three years! For three years I wasn't allowed to see my friends, or my family . . . It was not considered proper for a young married virgin to spend time with other married women. Such rubbish! I had to sleep in the same room as your mother, who kept watch over me, or rather my chastity. And it all seemed so normal, so natural to everyone. To me, too! I didn't even know how lonely I was. At night I slept with your mother, in the daytime I talked to your father. Thank God he was there. What a man! He was all

I had. And your mother hated that. She would get all wound up whenever she saw me with him. She used to send me straight to the kitchen. Your father read me poems, and told me stories. He encouraged me to read, and write, and think. He loved me. Because he loved you. He was proud of you, when you were fighting for freedom. He told me so. It was after freedom came that he started to hate you – you, and also your brothers, now that you were all fighting for nothing but power.'

Children's shouts ring out again on the rubble. The noise floods into the courtyard, and the house.

She falls silent. Listens to the children, who are playing the same game:

'Hadji mor'alé?'

'Balé?'

'Who wants the foot? Who wants the head?'

'I want the foot.'

They run off into the street again.

She takes up her story. 'Why was I talking about your father?' Rubs her head against the wall, seeming to think, to scour her memory . . . 'Yes, that's right, I was talking about the two of us, our marriage, my loneliness . . . Three years of waiting, and then you come home. I remember it like it was yesterday.

55

The day you came back, the day I saw you for the first time . . .' A sarcastic laugh bursts from her chest. 'You were just like you are now, not a word, not a glance . . .' Her eyes come to rest on the photo of the man. 'You sat down next to me. As if we already knew each other . . . as if you were seeing me after just a brief absence or I were some tawdry reward for your triumph! I was looking at you, but you were staring into thin air. I still don't know if it was modesty or pride. It doesn't matter. But I saw you, I watched you, I kept glancing at you, observing you. Noticing the slightest movement of your body, the slightest expression in your face . . .' Her right hand plays with the man's filthy hair. 'And you seemed so arrogant, so absent; you just weren't there. That saying is so true: "*One should never rely on a man who has known the pleasure of weapons!*"' She laughs again, but gently this time. 'Weapons become everything to you men . . . You must know that story about the military camp where an officer tries to demonstrate the value of a gun to the new recruits. He asks a young soldier, Benam, *Do you know what you have on your shoulder?* Benam replies, *Yes, Sir, it's my gun!* The officer yells back, *No, you moron! It's your mother, your sister, your honour!* Then he moves on to the next soldier

56

and asks him the same question. The soldier responds, *Yes, Sir! It's Benam's mother, and sister, and honour!*' She is still laughing. 'That story is so true. You men! As soon as you have guns, you forget your women.' She sinks back into silence, still stroking the man's hair. Tenderly. For a long time.

Then she continues, her voice sad. 'When I got engaged, I knew nothing of men. Nothing of married life. I knew only my parents. And what an example! All my dad cared about were his quails, his fighting quails! I often saw him kissing those quails, but never my mother, nor us, his children. There were seven of us. Seven girls starved of affection.' She stares at the frozen flight of the migrating birds on the curtains. Sees her father: 'He always used to sit cross-legged. He would be wearing his tunic, holding the quail in his left hand and stroking it at just the level of his thing, with its little feet poking through his hand; with the other hand, he would caress its neck in the most obscene way. For hours and hours on end! Even when he had visitors he didn't stop performing his *gassaw*, as he called it. It was a kind of prayer for him. He was so proud of his quails. Once, when it was bitterly, freezing cold, I even saw him tucking one of the quails under his trousers, into his *kheshtak*. I was little. For a long time after that I thought that men had quails between their legs! Thinking about it used to make me laugh. Imagine my disappointment, when I saw your balls for the first time.' A smile interrupts her and she closes her eyes. Her left hand strays into her own loosened hair, caressing the roots. 'I hated his quails.' She opens her eyes. Her sad gaze loses itself once more in the hole-studded sky of the curtains. 'Every Friday, he used to take them to the fight in the Qaf gardens. He would place bets. Sometimes he won, sometimes he lost. When he lost he would get upset, and nasty. He would come home in a rage and find any pretext to beat us . . . and also my mother.' She stops herself. The pain stops her. A pain that spreads to the tips of her fingers and digs them more deeply into the roots of her black hair. She forces herself to carry on. 'He must have won a lot of money in one of those fights . . . but then he put everything he had into buying a hugely expensive quail. He spent weeks and weeks getting it ready for a very important fight. And . . .' She laughs, a bitter laugh that contains both sarcasm and despair, and continues. 'As fate would have it, he lost. He had no money left to honour his bet, so he gave my sister instead. At twelve years old, my sister was sent to live with a man of forty!' Her nails leave the roots of her hair, and move down her forehead to finger the scar at the edge of her left eye. 'At the time, I was only ten . . . no . . .' She thinks about it. 'Yes, ten years old. I was scared. Scared that I too would become the stakes of a bet. So, do you know what I did with the quail?' She pauses a moment. It is unclear whether this is to make her story more exciting, or because she is afraid to reveal the next part. Eventually, she continues. 'One day . . . it was a Friday, while he was at the mosque for prayers before going to the Qaf gardens, I got the bird out of its cage, and set it free just as a stray cat – a ginger and white tabby – was keeping watch on the wall.' She takes a deep breath. 'And the cat caught it. He took it into a corner to eat it in peace. I followed. I stood there watching. I have never forgotten that moment. I even wished the cat "*bon appétit*". I was happy, thrilled to watch that cat eat the quail. A moment of pure delight. But very soon, I started to feel jealous. I wanted to be the cat, this cat savouring my father's quail. I was jealous, and sad. The cat knew nothing of the quail's worth. It couldn't share my joy, my triumph. "What a waste!" I thought to myself, and suddenly rushed over to grab what was left of the bird. The cat scratched my face and scurried off with the quail. I felt so frustrated and desperate that I started licking the floor like a fly, licking up those few drops of blood from my father's quail that had dripped on to the floor.' Her lips grimace. As if still tasting the warm wetness of the blood. 'When my father came home and found the cage empty, he went mad. Out of his mind. He was screaming. He beat up my mother, my sisters and me, because we hadn't kept watch over his quail. His bloody quail! While he was beating me, I shouted that it was good riddance, because that bloody quail had sent my sister away. My father understood immediately. He shut me in the cellar. It was dark. I had to spend two days in there. He left a cat with me – another stray who must have been roaming around – and told me glee-fully that if the animal got hungry it would eat me. But luckily, our house was full of rats. So the cat became my friend.' She stops, shakes off her memories of the cellar, and comes back to the room, and her man. Unsettled, she gazes at him a while, and suddenly moves away from the wall. 'But . . . but why am I telling him all this?' she murmurs. Overcome by her memories, she stands up heavily. 'I never wanted anyone to know that. Never! Not even my sisters!' She leaves the room, upset. Her fears echo down the passage. 'He's driving me mad. Sapping my strength. Forcing me to speak. To confess my sins, my mistakes. He's listening to me. Hearing me. I'm sure of it. He wants to get to me . . . to destroy me!'

She shuts herself into one of the other rooms, to calm her nerves with total solitude.

The children are still shouting among the ruins.

The sun moves over to the other side of the house, withdrawing its rays of light from the holes in the yellow and blue sky of the curtains.

Later, she comes back. Eyes solemn, hands shaking. She walks up to the man. Stops. Takes a deep breath. Grabs hold of the feeding tube. Closes her eyes and pulls it out of his mouth. Turns around, her eyes still closed. Takes an uncertain step. Sobs 'Forgive me, God!', picks up her veil and disappears.

She runs. Through the garden. Down the street . . .

The sugar-salt solution drips, one drop at a time, from the hanging tube on to the man's forehead. It flows into the valleys of his wrinkles, then towards the base of his nose, into his eye sockets, across his chapped cheeks, and finally into his thick, bushy moustache.

The sun is setting.

The weapons awakening.

Tonight again they will destroy.

Tonight again they will kill.

Morning.

Rain.

Rain on the city and its rubble.

Rain on the bodies and their wounds.

A few breaths after the last drop of sugar-salt solution, the sound of wet footsteps slaps through the courtyard, and into the passage. The muddy shoes are not removed.

The door to the room creaks open. It's the woman. She doesn't dare enter. She observes the man with that strange, wary look in her eyes. Pushes the door a fraction wider. Waits some more. Nothing moves. She takes off her shoes and slips quietly in, remaining on the threshold. She lets her veil fall to the floor. She is shaking. With cold. Or fear. She walks forward, until her feet are touching the mattress on which the man is lying.

The breathing has its usual rhythm.

The mouth is still half-open.

The look is still mocking.

The eyes are still empty, soulless . . . but today

they are wet with tears. She crouches down, terrified. 'Are you . . . are you crying?' She sinks to the ground. But soon realises that the tears come from the tube; they are sugar-salt tears.

Her throat is dry, her voice deadened. Blank. 'But, who are you?' A moment goes by – two breaths. 'Why doesn't God send Ezraeel, to finish you off once and for all?' she asks suddenly. 'What does he want from you?' She looks up. 'What does he want from me?' Her voice drops. 'You would say, *He wants to punish you!*' She shakes her head. 'Don't kid yourself!' Her voice is clearer now. 'Perhaps it's you he wants to punish! He's keeping you alive so you can see what I'm capable of doing with you, to you. He is making me into a demon . . . a demon for you, against you! Yes, I am your demon! In flesh and blood!' She lies down on the mattress to avoid the man's glassy stare. Lies there a long moment, silent and thoughtful. Travelling far, far back into the past, to the day the demon was born in her.

'After everything I confessed yesterday, you would tell me I was already a demon as a young child. A demon in my father's eyes.' Her hand touches the man's arm tenderly. Strokes it. 'But I was never a demon to you, was I?' She shakes her head. 'Or maybe I was . . .' Her silence is full of doubt and uncertainty. 'But everything I did was for you . . . in order to keep you.' Her hand slips on to the man's chest. 'Or actually, to tell you the truth, so that you would keep me. So that you wouldn't leave me! Yes, that's why I . . .' She stops herself. Draws in her knees and curls up on her side, next to the man. 'I did everything I could to make you stay with me. Not just because I loved you, but so that you wouldn't abandon me. Without you, I didn't have anyone. They would all have sent me packing.' She falls silent. Scratches her head. 'I admit that to start with I wasn't very sure of myself. Wasn't sure I could love you. I didn't know how to love a hero. It seemed so out of reach somehow, like a dream. For three years, I had been trying to imagine what you were like . . . and then one day you came. You slipped into the bed. Climbed on top of me. Rubbed yourself against me . . . and couldn't do it! And you didn't even dare say a word to me. In total darkness, with our hearts beating furiously, our breathing all jerky, our bodies streaming with sweat . . .' Her eyes are closed. She is far away, far from this motionless body. Drowning in the darkness of that night of desire.

Of that hunger. She remains there a moment. Totally silent. Totally still.

Then: 'After that, I very quickly became used to you, to your clumsy body, your empty presence which at that point I didn't know how to inter-pret . . . and gradually, I started to worry when you went away. To keep watch for your return. I used to get in a terrible state when you went away, even for a little while . . . I felt as if something was missing. Not in the house, but inside of me . . . I felt empty. So I started to stuff myself with food. And each time, your mother would come over to me, asking impatiently whether I didn't feel nauseous at all. She thought I was pregnant! When I told other people – my sisters – about this distress, about the state I got into when you were away, they said I was just in love, that was all. But all that didn't last long. After about five or six months, everything changed. Your mother had decided I was barren, and kept hassling me all the time. And you did, too. But . . .' Her hand reaches up and swipes through the air above her head, as if to chase away the remaining words bent on attacking her.

A few moments later – five or six breaths – she continues: 'And you took up your gun again. Left again for that crazy fratricidal war! You became conceited, arrogant and violent! Like all your family, except your father. The others despised me, they all did. Your mother was dying to see you take a second wife. I soon realised what was in store for me. My fate. You know nothing . . . nothing of all I did, so that you would keep me.' She rests her head on the man's arm. A timid smile, as if to beg for his mercy. 'You will forgive me, one day, for all that I've done . . .' Her face closes. 'But when I think about it now . . . if you had known, you would have killed me straight away!' She leans right over the man and looks at him for a long time, staring into his vacant eyes. Then she rests her cheek tenderly on his chest. 'How strange this all is! I've never felt as close to you as I do right now. We've been married ten years. Ten years! And it's only these last three weeks that I'm finally sharing something with you.' Her hand strokes the man's hair. 'I can touch you . . . You never let me touch you, never!' She moves towards the man's mouth. 'I have never kissed you.' She kisses him. 'The first time I went to kiss you on the lips, you pushed me away. I wanted it to be like in those Indian films. Perhaps you were scared –

is that it?' she asks, looking amused. 'Yes. You were scared because you didn't know how to kiss a girl.' Her lips brush against the bushy beard. 'Now I can do anything I want with you!' She lifts her head, to get a better look at her vacant-eyed man. Stares at him a long time, close up. 'I can talk to you about anything, without being interrupted, or blamed!' She nuzzles her head into his shoulder. 'After I left, yesterday, I was filled with such a strange, indefinable feeling. I felt both sad and relieved, both happy and unhappy.' She stares into the thickness of his beard. 'Yes, a strange relief. I couldn't understand how, as well as feeling upset and horribly guilty, I could also feel relieved, as if a burden had been lifted. I wasn't sure if it was because of . . .' She stops. As always, it is difficult to know whether she is blocking out her thoughts, or groping for the right words.

She rests her head back on the man's chest, and continues. 'Yes, I thought that maybe I felt relieved because I had finally been able to desert you . . . to leave you to die . . . to rid myself of you!' She huddles into the man's motionless body, as if cold. 'Yes, rid myself of you . . . because yesterday, all of a sudden, I started thinking that you were still conscious, quite well in mind and body but determined to make me talk, to find out my secrets and possess me completely. So I was scared.' She kisses his chest. 'Can you forgive me?' She looks at him tenderly. 'I left the house, hidden beneath my chador, and wandered the streets of this deaf, blind city in tears. Like a madwoman! When I went back to my aunt's house in the evening, everyone thought I was ill. I went straight to my room to collapse into my distress, my guilt. I didn't sleep all night. I was sure I was a monster, a proper demon! I was terrorised. Had I lost my mind, become a criminal?' She pulls away from her man's body. 'Like you, like your cronies . . . like the men who beheaded the neighbour's whole family! Yes, I belonged to your camp. Coming to that conclusion was terrifying. I cried all night long.' She moves closer to him. 'Then, in the morning, at dawn, just before it started raining, the wind opened the window . . . I was cold . . . and afraid. I snuggled up to my girls . . . I felt a presence behind me. I didn't dare look. I felt a hand stroking me. I couldn't move. I heard my father's voice. I gathered every ounce of strength, and turned around. He was there. With his white beard. His little eyes blinking in the darkness. The worn-out shape of him. In his hands he was carrying the quail I had given to the cat. He claimed that everything

I told you yesterday had brought his quail back to life! Then he embraced me. I stood up. He wasn't there. Gone, taken by the wind. The rain. Was it a dream? No . . . it was so real! His breath on my neck, his calloused palm against my skin . . .' She rests her chin on her hand, to keep her head upright. 'I was thrilled by his visit, lit up. I finally realised that the cause of my relief was not my attempt to abandon you to death.' She stretches. 'Do you understand what I'm saying? . . . The thing that was actually releasing me was having talked about that business of the quail. The fact of having confessed it. Confessed all of it, to you. And then I realised that since you've been ill, since I've been talking to you, getting angry with you, insulting you, telling you everything that I've kept hidden in my heart, and you not being able to reply, or do anything at all . . . all of this has been soothing and comforting to me.' She grasps the man by the shoulders. 'So, if I feel relieved, set free – in spite of the terrible things that keep happening to us – it is thanks to my secrets, and to you. I am not a demon!' She lets go of his shoulders, and strokes his beard. 'Because now your body is mine, and my secrets are yours. You are here for me. I don't know whether you can see or not, but one thing I am absolutely sure of is that you can hear me, that you can understand what I'm saying. And that is why you're still alive. Yes, you are alive for my sake, for the sake of my secrets.' She shakes him. 'You'll see. Just as my secrets were able to resuscitate my father's quail, they will bring you back to life! Look, it's been three weeks now that you've been living with a bullet in your neck. That's totally unheard of! No one can believe it, no one! You don't eat, you don't drink and yet you're still here! It's a miracle. A miracle for me, and thanks to me. Your breath hangs on the telling of my secrets.' She gets to her feet with ease and then stands over him, full of grace, as if to say: 'Don't worry, there is no end to my secrets.' Her words can be heard through the door. 'I no longer want to lose you!'

She returns to refill the drip bag. 'Now I finally understand what your father was saying about that sacred stone. It was near the end of his life. You were away, you'd gone off to war again. It was a few months ago, just before you were hit by this bullet, your father was ill, and I was the only one looking after him. He was obsessed by a magic stone. A black stone. He talked about it the whole time . . . What did he call that stone?' She tries to think of the word. 'He asked every friend who visited to bring him this stone . . . a precious, black stone . . .' She inserts the tube into the man's throat. 'You know, that stone you put in front of you . . . and tell all your problems to, all your struggles, all your pain, all your woes . . . to which you confess everything in your heart, everything you don't dare tell anyone . . .' She checks the drip. 'You talk to it, and talk to it. And the stone listens, absorbing all your words, all your secrets, until one fine day it explodes. Shatters into tiny pieces.' She cleans and moistens the man's eyes. 'And on that day you are set free from all your pain, all your suffering . . . What's that stone called?' She rearranges the sheet. 'The day before he died, your father called for me, he wanted to see me alone. He was dying. He whispered to me, "*Daughter, the angel of death has appeared to me, accompanied by the angel Gabriel, who revealed a secret that I am entrusting to you. I now know where this stone is to be found. It is in the Ka'bah, in Mecca! In the house of God! You know, that Black Stone around which millions of pilgrims circle during the big Eid celebrations. Well, that's the very stone I was telling you about . . . In heaven, this stone served as a throne for Adam . . . but after God banished Adam and Eve to earth, he sent it down too, so that Adam's children* could tell it of their problems and sufferings . . . And it is this same stone that the angel Gabriel gave to Hagar and her son Ismael to use as a pillow when Abraham had banished the servant and her son into the desert . . . yes, it is a stone for all the world's unfortunates. Go there! Tell it your secrets until it bursts . . . until you are set free from your torments.'" Her lips turn ash-grey with sadness. She sits a moment in the silence of mourning.

Her voice husky, she continues. 'Pilgrims have been going to Mecca for centuries and centuries to circle around that stone, praying; so how come it hasn't exploded yet?' A sardonic laugh makes her voice ring out, and her lips regain their colour. 'It will explode one day, and that day will be the end of the world. Perhaps that's the nature of the Apocalypse.'

Someone is walking through the courtyard. She falls silent. The steps move further away. She carries on. 'Do you know what? . . . I think I have found that magic stone . . . my own magic stone.' The voices emanating from the ruins of the neighbouring house prevent her once more from pursuing her thoughts. She stands up nervously and goes to the window. Opens the curtains. She is petrified by what she sees. Her hand goes to her mouth. She doesn't make a sound. She closes the curtains, and watches the scene through the holes in the yellow and blue sky. 'They are burying the dead in their own garden,' she exclaims. 'Where is the old lady?' She stands quite still for a long moment. Overwhelmed, she turns back to her man. Lies down on the mattress, her head against his. Hides her eyes in the crook of her arm, breathing deeply and silently, as before. To the same rhythm as the man.

The voice of the Mullah reciting burial verses from the Koran is drowned out by the rain. The Mullah raises his voice and speeds up the prayer, to get it over with as quickly as possible.

The noise and whispering disperse across the sodden ruins.

Someone is walking towards the house. Now he is behind the door. Knocking. The woman doesn't move. More knocking. 'Is anyone there? It's me, the Mullah,' he shouts impatiently. The woman, deaf to his cry, still doesn't move. The Mullah mutters a few words and leaves. She sits back up and leans against the wall, keeping quite still until the Mullah's wet footsteps have disappeared down the street.

'I have to go to my aunt's place. I need to be with the children!' She gets to her feet. Stands there a moment, just long enough to listen to a few of the man's breaths.

Before she has picked up her veil, these words burst from her mouth: '*Sang-e sabur!*' She jumps. 'That's the name of the stone, *sang-e sabur*, the patience stone! The magic stone!' She crouches down next to the man. 'Yes, you, you are my *sang-e sabur*!' She strokes his face gently, as if actually touching a precious stone. 'I'm going to tell you everything, my *sang-e sabur*. Everything. Until I set myself free from my pain, and my suffering, and until you, you . . .' She leaves the rest unsaid. Letting the man imagine it.

She leaves the room, the passage, the house . . .

Ten breaths later she is back, out of breath. She drops her wet veil on the floor and rushes up to the man. 'They'll be patrolling again tonight – the other side this time, I think. Searching all the houses . . . They mustn't find you . . . They'll kill you!' She kneels down, stares at him close up. 'I won't let them! I need you now, my *sang-e sabur*!' She walks to the door, says 'I'm going to get the cellar ready', and leaves the room.

A door creaks. Her steps ring out on the stairs. Suddenly she cries desperately, 'Oh no! Not this!' She comes back up, in a panic. 'The cellar has flooded!' Paces up and down. Her hand to her forehead, as if rummaging through her memories for somewhere to hide her man. Nothing. So it will have to be here, in this room. Determined, she snatches the green curtain and pulls it aside. It's a junk room, full of pillows, blankets and piled-up mattresses.

Having emptied the space, she lays out a mattress. Too big. She folds it over and scatters the cushions around it. Takes a step back to get a better sense of her work – the nook for her precious stone. Satisfied, she walks back over to the man. With great care, she pulls the tube out of his mouth, takes him by the shoulders, lifts him up, drags the body over and slides it on to the mattress. She arranges him so that he's almost sitting up, wedged in by cushions, facing the entrance to the room. The man's expressionless gaze is still frozen, somewhere on the kilim. She reattaches the drip bag to the wall, inserts the tube back into his mouth, closes the green curtain and conceals the hiding place with the other mattresses and blankets. You would never know there was anyone there.

'I'll be back tomorrow,' she whispers. She is in the doorway, leaning down to pick up her veil, when a sudden gunshot, not far away, rivets her to the floor, freezing her mid-movement. A second shot, even closer. A third . . . and then shots ringing out from all directions, going in all directions.

Sitting on the floor, her wails of 'my children . . .' reach no one; they are drowned out by the dull rumblings of a tank.

Bent double, she makes her way to the window. Peeks outside, through the holes in the curtain, and is filled with despair. A tear-soaked cry bursts from her chest, 'Protect us, God!'

She sits against the wall between the two windows, just beneath the khanjar and the photo of her mocking man.

She is groaning, quietly.

Somebody shoots right next to the house. He is probably inside the courtyard, posted behind the wall. The woman chokes back her tears, her breath. She lifts the bottom of the curtain. Seeing a shape shooting towards the street, she moves sharply back, and cautiously makes her way over to the door.

In the passage, the silhouette of an armed man makes her freeze. 'Get back in the room!' She goes back into the room. 'Sit down and don't move!' She sits down where her man used to lie, and does not move. The man emerges from the dark passage, wearing a turban with a length of it concealing half his face. He fills the doorway, and dominates the room. Through the narrow gap in his turban his dark gaze sweeps the space. Without a word, he moves over to the window and glances out towards the street, where shots are still being fired. He turns back towards the woman to reassure her: 'Don't be afraid, sister. I will protect you.' Once again, he surveys his surroundings. She is not afraid, just desperate. And yet she manages to act serene, sure of herself.

Sitting between the two men, one hidden by a black turban, the other by a green curtain, her eyes flicker with nerves.

The armed man crouches on his heels, his finger on the trigger.

Still suspicious and on edge, he looks away from the curtains towards the woman, and asks her, 'Are you alone?' In a calm voice – too calm – she replies,

'No.' Pauses a moment, then continues fervently, 'Allah is with me', pauses again, and glances at the green curtain.

The man is silent. He is glaring at the woman.

Outside, the shooting has stopped. All that can be heard, in the distance, is the dull roar of the tank leaving.

The room, the courtyard and the street sink into a heavy, smoky silence.

The sound of footsteps makes the man jump and he turns his gun on her, gesturing to her not to move. He peers through a hole in the curtain. His tensed shoulders relax. He is relieved. He lifts the curtain a fraction and hisses a code in a low voice. The steps pause. The man whispers, 'Hey, it's me. Come in!'

The other man enters the room. He too is wearing a turban with a part of it hiding his face. His thin, lanky body is wrapped in a *patou* – a long, heavy woollen shawl. Surprised by the woman's presence, he crouches down next to his companion, who asks him, 'So?' The second man's eyes are fixed on the woman as he replies, 'It's ok-ok-okay, th-the there's a c-c-ceasefire!', stammering, his voice a teenager's in the process of breaking.

'Until when?'

'I . . . I . . . d-d-d-don't know!' he replies, still distracted by the woman's presence.

'Okay, now get out of here and keep watch! We're staying here tonight.'

The young man doesn't protest. Still staring at the woman, he asks for 'a c-c-c-cigarette', which the first chucks over to get rid of him as quickly as possible. Then, having completely uncovered his bearded face, he lights up himself.

The boy darts a final stunned glance at the woman from the doorway, and reluctantly disappears down the passage.

The woman stays where she is. She observes the man's every movement with a distrust she is still attempting to hide. 'Are you not afraid of being all alone?' the man asks, exhaling smoke. She shrugs her shoulders. 'Do I have any choice?' After another long drag, the man asks, 'Don't you have anyone to look after you?' The woman glances at the green curtain. 'No, I'm a widow!'

'Which side?'

'Yours, I presume.'

The man doesn't push it. He takes another deep drag, and asks, 'Have you any children?'

'Yes. Two . . . two girls.'

'Where are they?'

'With my aunt.'

'And you – why are you here?'

'To work. I need to earn my living, so I can feed my two kids.'

'And what do you do for work?'

The woman looks him straight in the eye, and says it: 'I earn my living by the sweat of my body.'

'What?' he asks, confused.

The woman replies, her voice shameless: 'I sell my body.'

'What bullshit is this?'

'I sell my body, as you sell your blood.'

'What are you on about?'

'I sell my body for the pleasure of men!'

Overcome with rage, the man spits, '*Allah, Al-Rahman! Al-Mu'min!* Protect me!'

'Against who?'

The cigarette smoke spews out of the man's mouth as he continues to invoke his God, 'In the name of Allah!', to drive away the devil, 'Protect me from Satan!', then takes another huge drag to belch out alongside words of fury, 'But aren't you ashamed to say this?!'

'To say it, or to do it?'

'Are you a Muslim, or aren't you?'

'I'm a Muslim.'

'You will be stoned to death! You'll be burnt alive in the flames of hell!'

He stands up and recites a long verse from the Koran. The woman is still sitting. Her gaze is scornful. Defiantly, she looks him up and down, from head to foot, and foot to head. He is spitting. The smoke of his cigarette veils the fury of his beard, the blackness of his eyes. He moves forward with a dark look. Pointing his gun at the woman, he bawls, 'I'm going to kill you, whore!' The barrel sits on her belly. 'I'm going to explode your filthy cunt! Dirty whore! Devil!' He spits on her face. The woman doesn't move. She scoffs at the man. Impassive, she seems to be daring him to shoot.

The man clenches his teeth, gives a great yell and leaves the house.

The woman remains motionless until she hears the man reach the courtyard, and call out to the other, 'Come on, we're getting out of here. This is an ungodly house!' Until she hears the flight of their footsteps down the muddy road.

She closes her eyes, sighs, breathes out the smoky air she has been holding in her lungs for a long time. A triumphant smile flickers across her dry lips. After a long gaze at the green curtain, she unfolds her body and moves over to her man. 'Forgive me!' she whispers. 'I had to tell him that – otherwise, he would have raped me.' She is shaken by a sarcastic laugh. 'For men like him, to fuck or rape a whore is not an achievement. Putting his filth into a hole that has already served hundreds before him does not engender the slightest masculine pride. Isn't that right, my *sang-e sabur*? You should know. Men like him are afraid of whores. And do you know why? I'll tell you, my *sang-e sabur*: when you fuck a whore, you don't dominate her body. It's a matter of exchange. You give her money, and she gives you pleasure. And I can tell you that often she's the dominant one. It's she who is fucking you.' The woman calms down. Her voice serene, she continues, 'So, raping a whore is not rape. But raping a young girl's virginity, a woman's honour! Now that's your creed!' She stops, leaving a long moment of silence for her man – if he can, and she hopes he can – to think about her words.

'Don't you agree, my *sang-e sabur*?' she continues. She approaches the curtain, moving aside some of the mattresses concealing the hiding place. She looks deep into her man's glassy eyes, and says, 'I do hope you're managing to grasp and absorb everything I'm telling you, my *sang-e sabur*.' Her head is poking slightly through the curtain. 'Perhaps you're wondering where I could have picked all this up! Oh my *sang-e sabur*, I've still so much to tell you . . .' She moves back. 'Things that have been stored up inside me for a while now. We've never had the chance to discuss them. Or – let's be honest – you've never given me the chance.' She pauses, for one breath, asking herself where and how she should start. But the Mullah's cry, calling the faithful to prostrate them-selves before their God at twilight, throws her into a panic and drives her secrets back inside. She stands up suddenly: 'May God cut off my tongue! It's about to get dark! My children!' She rushes over to lift the curtains patterned with migrating birds. Behind the grey veil of the rain, everything has been plunged once more into a gloomy darkness.

By the time she has made a final check of the gaps between the drops of sugar-salt solution, picked up her veil, closed the doors and reached the courtyard, it's already too late. Now that the call to prayer is complete, the Mullah announces the neighbourhood curfew and asks everyone to respect the ceasefire.

The woman's footsteps pause on the wet ground.

They hesitate.

They are lost.

They go back the way they came.

The woman comes back into the room.

Upset, she drops her veil on the floor and lets herself fall, wearily, on to the mattress previously occupied by the body of her man. 'I leave my daughters in Allah's hands!' She recites a verse from the Koran, trying to persuade herself of God's power to protect her girls. Then she lies down, abandoning herself to the darkness of the room. Her eyes manage to see through the dark towards the mattresses. Behind the mattresses, the green curtain. Behind the curtain, her man, her *sang-e sabur.*

A gunshot, far away. Then another, close. And thus ceases the ceasefire.

The woman stands up, and walks towards the plain green curtain. She pushes the mattresses aside, but doesn't open the curtain. 'So I'll have to stay here. I've a whole night to myself, to talk to you, my *sang-e sabur.* Anyway, what was I saying before that stupid Mullah started screeching?' She makes herself focus. 'Oh yes, you were wondering where I could have got all these notions. That was it, wasn't it? I have had two teachers in my life – my aunt and your father. My aunt taught me how to live with men, and your father taught me why. My aunt . . .' she opens the curtain slightly. 'You didn't know her at all. And thank God! You would have sent her packing straight away. Now I can tell you every-thing. She is my father's only sister. What a woman! I grew up enveloped in her warmth. I loved her more than my own mother. She was generous. Beautiful. Very beautiful. Big hearted. She was the one who taught me how to read, how to live . . . but then her life took a tragic turn. They married her off to this terrible rich man. A total bastard. Stuffed with dirty cash. After two years of marriage, my aunt hadn't been able to bear a child for him. I say for him, because that's how you men see it. Anyway, my aunt was infertile. In other words, no good. So her husband sent her to his parents' place in the countryside, to be their servant. As she was both beautiful and infertile, her father-in-law used to fuck her without a care in the world. Day and night. Eventually, she cracked. Bashed his head in. They threw her out of her in-laws' house. Her husband sent her away, too. She was abandoned by her own family – including my father. So, as the "black sheep" of the family, she vanished, leaving a note saying she had put an end to her days. Sacrificed her body, reduced it to ashes! Leaving no trace. No grave. And of course, this suited everyone just fine. No funeral. No service for that "witch"! I was the only one who cried. I was fourteen years old at the time. I used to think about her constantly.' She stops, bows her head, closes her eyes as if dreaming of her.

After a few breaths, she starts up again, as if in a trance. 'One day, more than seven years ago, just before you came back from the war, I was strolling around the market with your mother. I stopped at the underwear stall. Suddenly, a voice I knew. I turned around. There was my aunt! For a moment I thought I was seeing things. But it really was her. I greeted her, but she acted as if she hadn't heard, as if she didn't know me. And yet I was absolutely, one hundred percent sure. I knew in my blood that it was her. So I managed to lose your mother in the crowd. Began trailing my aunt. I didn't let her out of my sight, all the way to her house. I stopped her at her front door. She burst into tears. Gave me a big hug, and asked me in. At the time she was living in a brothel.' She falls silent, giving her man, behind the green curtain, the chance to take a few breaths. And herself, too.

In the city, the shooting continues. Far away, nearby, sporadic.

In the room, everything is sunk in darkness.

Saying 'I'm hungry', she stands up and feels her way into the passage, and then into the kitchen to find something to eat. First she kindles a lamp, which brightens part of the passage and sheds a little light into the room as well. Then, after the slamming of a few cupboard doors, she returns. A hard crust of several-day-old bread and an onion in one hand, the hurricane lamp in the other. She sits back down near her man, by the green curtain which she pulls aside in the yellowish lamplight to check that her *sang-e sabur* has not exploded. No.

It is still there. In one piece. Eyes open. Mocking expression, even with the tube thrust into the pathetically half-open mouth. The chest continues, miraculously, to rise and fall at the same pace as before.

'And now, it's that aunt who has taken me in. She likes my children. And the girls like her, too. That's why I'm slightly more relaxed.' She peels the onion. 'She tells them loads of stories . . . as she used to before. I grew up with her stories too.' She puts a layer of onion on a bit of bread, and shoves the whole thing into her mouth. The cracking of the dry bread mingles with the softness of her voice. 'The other night, she wanted to tell a particular story that her mother used to tell us. I begged her not to tell it to my girls. It's a very disturbing tale. Cruel. But full of power and magic! My girls are still too young to understand it.' She takes a sip from the glass of water she had brought to moisten her man's eyes.

'As you know, in my family we were all girls. Seven girls! And no boy! Our parents hated that. It was also the reason our grandmother told my sisters and me that story. For a long time, I thought she had invented it especially for us. But then my aunt told me that she had first heard that story from her great-grandmother.'

A second layer of onion on a second crust of bread.

'In any case, our grandmother warned us in advance, by telling us that the story was a magical tale that could bring us either happiness or misfortune in our actual lives. This warning frightened us, but it was also exciting. And so her lovely voice rang out to the frenetic beating of our hearts. *Once upon a time there was, or was not, a king. A charming king. A brave king. This king, however, had one constraint in his life – just one, but of the utmost importance: he was never to have a daughter. On his wedding night, the astrologers told him that if ever his wife should give birth to a girl, she would bring disgrace upon the crown. As fate would have it, his wife gave birth to nothing but girls. And so, at each birth, the king would order his executioner to kill the newborn baby!*'

Lost in her memories, the woman suddenly takes on the appearance of an old lady – her grandmother, no doubt – telling this story to her grandchildren.

'*The executioner killed the first baby girl, and the second. With the third, he was stopped by a little voice emanating from the mouth of the*

89

newborn. It begged him to tell her mother that if she kept her alive, the queen would have her own kingdom! Troubled by these words, the executioner visited the queen in secret, and told her what he had seen and heard. The queen, not breathing a word to the king, immediately came to take a look at this newborn with the gift of speech. Full of wonder yet terrified, she asked the executioner to prepare a cart so they could flee the country. At exactly midnight, the queen, her daughter and the executioner secretly left the city for distant lands.'

Nothing distracts her from her tale, not even the shots fired not far from the house. *'Furious at this sudden flight and determined to see his wife again, the king departed in conquest of foreign lands.* Grandmother always used to pause at exactly this point in the story. She would always ask the same question: *But was it to see his wife again, or to track her down?'*

She smiles. In just the way her grandmother smiled, perhaps. And continues:

'The years went by. During one of these war-mongering trips, the king was resisted by a small kingdom governed by a brave, fair and peaceful queen. The people refused the interference of this foreign king. This arrogant king! So, the king decreed

*that the country be burned to the ground. The
queen's advisors counselled her to meet the king
and negotiate with him. But the queen was against
this meeting. She said she would rather set fire to
the country herself than attend the negotiation. And
so her daughter – who was much loved by the court
and the people not only for her remarkable beauty
but also her outstanding intelligence and kindness
– asked her mother if she could meet the king herself.
On hearing her daughter's request, the queen seemed
to lose her mind. She began screaming, cursing the
entire world at the top of her voice. She no longer
slept. She wandered the palace. She forbade her
daughter to leave her bedroom, or to take any
action. Nobody could understand her. With every
day that passed, the kingdom sank a little deeper
into catastrophe. Food and water became scarce. At
this point the daughter, who could understand her
mother no better than anyone else, decided to meet
the king despite the prohibition. One night, with
the help of her confidant, she made her way to the
king's tent. On seeing her heavenly beauty, the king
fell madly in love with the princess. He made her
the following offer: if she would marry him, he
would renounce his claim to the kingdom. The
princess accepted, somewhat entranced herself. They*

spent the night together. In the early hours, she made her triumphant way back to the palace, to tell her mother about this encounter with the king. Luckily, she didn't admit that she had also spent the night in his tent. When she heard her daughter had so much as seen the king, the queen succumbed to absolute despair. She was willing to face any ordeal life could throw at her, except this one! Overcome, she howled, "Fate! Oh cursed fate!" and fainted. Still understanding nothing of what was going on inside her mother's head, the daughter spoke to the man who had been at her mother's side throughout her life, and asked him the cause of the queen's distress. And so he told her this story. "Dear princess, as you know, I am not your father. The truth is that you are the daughter of this swaggering king! As for me, I was only his executioner." He told her everything that had happened, finishing with this enigmatic conclusion: "And this, my princess, is our fate. If we tell the king the truth, the law decrees that all three of us shall be sentenced to hang. And all the people of this kingdom shall become his slaves. If we oppose his intentions, our kingdom shall be burned down. And if you marry him, you shall be committing the unpardonable sin of incest! All of us shall be cursed and punished by God."

Grandmother used to stop at this point in the story. We would ask her to tell us what happened next, and she would say: *Unfortunately, my little girls, I don't know how the story ends. To this day, nobody knows. They say that the man or woman who discovers the end of the story shall be protected from hardship for the rest of their life.* Not fully convinced, I would object that, if no one knew the end of the story, how could anyone tell if an ending was right? She used to laugh sadly and kiss me on the forehead. *That's what we call mystery, my dear. Any ending is possible, but to know which is the right ending, the fair ending . . . now that is the preserve of mystery.* At that point, I used to ask her if it was a true story. She would reply, *I told you, "Once upon a time there was, or was not" . . .* My question was the same question she, as a young girl, used to ask her own grandmother, and to which her grandmother would reply, *And that is the mystery, my dear; that is the mystery.* That story haunted me for years. It used to keep me awake at night. Every night, in bed, I would plead with God to whisper the end of the story to me! A happy ending, so that I could have a happy life! I would make up all kinds of stuff in my head. As soon as I came up with an idea, I would rush to tell my grandmother. And she would shrug her shoulders and say, *It's possible, my dear. It's possible. Your life will reveal whether you are right or not. It's your life that will confirm it. But whatever you discover, never tell anyone. Never! Because, as in any magical tale, whatever you say may come to pass. So, make sure to keep this ending to yourself.'*

She eats. A crust of bread, a layer of onion. 'Once, I asked your father if he knew the story. He said no. So I told it to him. At the end, he paused a long while, then said these poignant words: *You know, my daughter, it's an illusion to think you can find a happy ending to this story. It's impossible. Incest has been committed, and so tragedy is inevitable.'*

In the street, we hear someone shouting, 'Halt!' And then a gunshot.

And footsteps, fleeing.

The woman continues. 'So, your father disabused me of my illusions. But a few days later, when I brought him his breakfast early one morning, he asked me to sit down so we could talk about the story. Speaking very slowly and deliberately, he said, *My daughter, I have thought long and hard. And actually, there could be a happy ending.* I was so

94

keen to hear this ending that I felt like throwing myself into his arms, kissing his hands and feet. I restrained myself, of course. I forgot your mother and her breakfast, and sat down next to him. At that moment, my whole body was one giant ear, ignoring all other voices, all other sounds. There was only the wise, trembling voice of your father, who after a great slurp of tea said the following: *As in life, my daughter, for this story to have a happy ending there must be a sacrifice. In other words, somebody's misfortune. Never forget, every piece of happiness must be paid for by two misfortunes.* "But why?" I asked with naïve surprise. He replied in simple words: *My daughter, unfortunately, or perhaps fortunately, not everyone in the world can attain happiness, in real life or in a story. The happiness of some engenders the hardship of others. It's sad, but true. So, in this story, you need misfortune and sacrifice in order to arrive at a happy ending. But your self-regard, and your care for your loved ones, prevents you from considering this. The story requires a murder. But who must be killed? Before replying, before killing anyone, you must ask yourself another question: who do you wish to see happy, and alive? The father-king? The mother-queen? Or the daughter-princess? As soon as you ask yourself this question, my daughter, everything changes. In the story and in you. For this to happen you must rid yourself of three loves, love of yourself, love of the father and love of the mother!* I asked him why. He looked at me quietly for a long time, his pale eyes shining behind his glasses. He must have been searching for words I would be able to understand. *If you are on the daughter's side, your love for yourself prevents you from imagining the daughter's suicide. In the same way, love for the father doesn't allow you to imagine that the daughter could accept the marriage and then kill her own father in the marital bed on the wedding night. Finally, love for the mother stops you from considering the murder of the queen in order that the daughter can live with the king and conceal the truth from him.* He let me think for a few moments. He took another long sip of tea and continued: *In the same way, if I, as a father, imagined an end to this story, it would be the strict application of the law. I would order the beheading of the queen, the princess and the executioner, to ensure that the traitors were punished and the secret of the incest buried for ever more.* "And what would the mother suggest?" I asked him. With a small private smile, he replied, *My daughter, I know nothing of maternal love, so I cannot give you her answer. You yourself are a mother now; it's for you to tell me. But my experiences in life tell me that a woman like the queen would rather have her kingdom destroyed and her people enslaved than reveal her secret. The mother behaves in a moral way. She will not allow her daughter to marry her father.* My God, it was hard, listening to those wise words. I was still desperately seeking a merciful outcome, and I asked him if this was at all possible. First of all he said yes – which comforted me – but then he shouted, *My daughter, tell me, who in this story has the power to forgive?* I replied naïvely, *The father.* Shaking his head, he said, *But, my daughter, the father – who has killed his own children, who during his warfaring has destroyed whole cities and populations, who has committed incest – the father is as guilty as the queen. As for her, she has betrayed the king and the law, certainly, but do not forget that she too was misled, by her newborn daughter and by the executioner.* Desperate, I concluded before I left, "So there is no happy ending!" *There is*, he said. *But, as I told you, it involves accepting a sacrifice, and renouncing three things, self-regard, the law of the father and the morality of the mother.* Stunned, I asked him if he thought that was feasible. His reply was very simple: *You must try, my daughter.* I was much affected by the discussion, and thought of little else for months. I came to realise that my distress came from one thing and one thing only – the truth of his words. Your father really knew something about life.'

Another crust of bread and layer of onion, swallowed with difficulty.

'The more I think of your father, the more I hate your mother. She kept him shut up in a small, sweaty room, sleeping on a rush mat. Your brothers treated him like a madman. Just because he had acquired great wisdom. Nobody understood him. To start with, I was afraid of him too. Not because of what your mother and brothers kept saying about him, but because I remembered what my aunt had suffered at the hands of her father-in-law. And yet, bit by bit I became closer to him. With a great deal of fear. But at the same time a shadowy, indefinable curiosity. An almost erotic curiosity! Perhaps it was the part of me haunted by my aunt that drew me to him. A desire to live the same things she had lived. Frightening, isn't it?'

Full of thoughts and emotion, she finishes her onion and stale bread.

She blows out the lamp.

She lies down.

And sleeps.

As the guns grow weary and quiet, the dawn arrives. Grey and silent.

A few breaths after the call to prayer, hesitant foot-steps can be heard on the muddy courtyard path. Someone reaches the house and knocks on the door to the passage. The woman opens her eyes. Waits. Again there is a knock. She stands up. Half asleep. Goes to the window to see who this person is who doesn't dare enter without knocking.

In the leaden fog of dawn, she makes out an armed, turbaned shadow. The woman's 'Yes?' draws the shape to the window. His face is hidden behind a length of turban; his voice, more fragile than his appearance, stammers, 'C-c-can I . . . c-c-come in?' It's the breaking teenage voice, the same one as yesterday. The woman tries to make out his features. But in the weak grey light she cannot be sure. She consents with a nod of the head, adding, 'The door is open.' She herself stays where she is, next to the window, watching the shadow as it moves along the walls, down the passage and into the doorway. The same clothing. The same way of hesitating on the threshold. The same timidity. It's him. No question. The same boy as the day before. She waits, quizzical. The boy is struggling to step into the room. Glued to the door frame, he tries to ask, 'How . . . m-m-much?' The woman can't understand a word he's saying.

'What do you want?'

'How . . .' The voice breaks. It picks up speed – 'How . . . m-m-much?' – but not clarity.

Holding her breath, the woman takes a step towards the boy. 'Listen, I'm not what you think I am. I . . .' She is interrupted by a cry from the boy, fierce to start with, 'Sh-sh-sh . . . shut up!', and then calm, 'How . . . m-m-much?' She tries to move back, but is halted by the barrel of the gun against her belly. Waiting for the boy to calm down, she says gently, 'I'm a mother . . .' But the boy's tense finger on the trigger prevents her from continuing. Resigned, she asks, 'How much do you have on you?' Trembling, he pulls a few notes from his pocket and throws them at her feet. The woman takes a step backwards and turns a little so she can cast a furtive glance at the hiding place. The green curtain is slightly open. But the darkness makes the man's presence imperceptible. She slips to the ground. Lying on her back, looking towards her man, she spreads her legs. And waits. The boy is paralysed. She cries impatiently: 'Come on then, let's get this over with!'

He puts his gun down next to the door, then, hesitantly, walks over, and stands above her. An inner turmoil has made his breathing all jerky. The woman closes her eyes.

Abruptly, he throws himself on top of her. The woman, struggling to breathe, gasps, 'Gently!' Overexcited, the boy awkwardly grabs hold of her legs. She is frozen, numb beneath the wild flapping of this clumsy young body as it tries vainly, head buried in her hair, to pull down her pants. She ends up doing it herself. Pulls his down, too. As soon as his penis brushes her thighs, he groans dully in the woman's hair; very pale, she keeps her eyes closed.

He is no longer moving. She neither.

He is breathing heavily. She too.

There is a moment of total stillness before a light breeze lifts and pulls apart the curtains. The woman opens her eyes at last. Her voice – weak but forgiving – whispers, 'Is it over?' The boy's wounded cry shocks her. 'Sh-sh-shut . . . sh-sh-sh-shut your mouth!' He doesn't dare raise his head, still buried in the woman's black hair. His breathing becomes less and less intense.

The woman, silent, gazes with infinite sadness at the gap in the green curtain.

The two entwined bodies remain still, fixed to the ground, for a little while longer. Then a new breeze creates a slight movement in this mass of flesh. It's the woman's hand that is moving. Gently stroking the boy.

He does not protest. She continues stroking. Tender and maternal. 'It doesn't matter,' she reassures him. No reaction at all from the boy. She perseveres: 'It can happen to anyone.' She is cautious. 'Is . . . is this the first time?' After a long silence, lasting three slow breaths, he nods his head – still sunk deep in the woman's hair – in shy, desperate assent. The woman's hand moves up to the boy's head, and touches his turban. 'You had to start somewhere.' She glances around to locate the gun. It is far away. Looks back at the boy who is still in the same position. She moves her legs a little. No protest. 'Right, shall we get up?' He doesn't reply. 'I told you, it doesn't matter . . . I'll help you.' Gently, she pushes up his right shoulder so she can shift on to her side and free herself of the boy's broken weight. Having done this, she attempts to pull up her knickers, first wiping her thighs with the hem of her dress. Then she sits up. The boy moves too, at last. Avoiding the woman's eyes, he pulls up his trousers and sits with his back to her, staring at his gun. His turban has come undone. His face is visible. He has large, pale eyes, outlined in smoky kohl. He is beautiful, his face thin and smooth. He has barely any facial hair. Or else he's very young. 'Do you have family?' the woman asks in a neutral voice. The boy shakes his head no, and quickly winds his turban back up, hiding half his face. Then, abruptly, he gets to his feet, grabs his gun and flees the house like lightning.

The woman is still sitting in the same place. She stays there a long time, without a glance at the green curtain. Her eyes fill with tears. Her body huddles up. She wraps her arms around her knees, tucks in her head and wails. A single, heartbreaking wail.

A breeze flutters, as if in response to her cry, lifting the curtains to let the grey fog flood the room.

The woman raises her head. Slowly. She does not stand. She still doesn't raise her eyes to the green curtain. She doesn't dare.

She stares down at the crumpled notes scattering in the breeze.

Cold or emotion, tears or terror make her breath come in gasps. She is shaking.

Eventually, she gets to her feet, and rushes into the passage, to the toilet. She washes, and changes her dress. Reappears. Dressed in green and white. Looking more serene.

She picks up the money and goes back to her spot by the hiding place. Pulls the curtain tight shut, without meeting the man's vacant eyes.

After a few silent breaths, a bitter laugh bursts from her guts, juddering her lips. 'So there you go . . . it doesn't just happen to other people! Sooner or later, it had to happen to us, too . . .'

She counts the notes, 'poor thing', and puts them in her pocket. 'Sometimes I think it must be hard to be a man. No?' She pauses for a moment. To think, or to wait for a reply. Starts again, with the same forced smile: 'That boy made me think about our own first times . . . if you don't mind me saying so. You know me . . . my memories always hit me just when I'm not expecting them. Or no longer expecting them. They plague me, I just can't help it. The good ones and the bad. It leads to some laughable moments. Like just now, when that boy was all distraught, and our first, belated honeymoon nights suddenly flashed into my brain . . . I swear, I didn't mean to think of you, it just happened. You were clumsy too, like that boy. Of course, at the time, I didn't know any better. I thought that was how it was supposed to be – how you did it. Although it often seemed to me that you weren't satisfied. And then I would feel guilty. I told myself that it was my fault, that I didn't know how to do it right. After a year, I discovered that actually, it was all coming from you. You gave nothing. Nothing. Remember all those nights when you fucked me and left me all . . . all keyed up . . . My aunt is quite right when she says that those who don't know how to make love, make war.' She won't let herself continue.

She pauses for a long time before saying, suddenly, 'Anyway, tell me, what is pleasure for you? Seeing your filth spurt? Seeing the blood spurt as you tear through the *virtuous veil?*'

She looks down, and bites her bottom lip. Furiously. The anger takes hold of her hand, grips it, turns it into a fist and crashes it against the wall. She groans.

Falls silent.

'Sorry! . . . This . . . this is the first time I've spoken to you like this . . . I'm ashamed of myself. I really don't know where it's all coming from. I never used to think about any of this before. I promise. Never!' A pause, then she continues. 'Even when I noticed that you were the only one whose pleasure peaked, it didn't bother me. On the contrary, I was pleased. I told myself it was normal. That it was the difference between us. You men take your pleasure, and we women derive ours from yours. That was enough for me. And it was my job and mine alone to give myself pleasure by . . . touching myself.' Her lip is bleeding. She blots it with her ring finger, then her tongue. 'One night, you caught me in the act. You were asleep. I had my back to you and was touching myself. Perhaps my panting woke you up. You jumped, and asked me what I was doing. I was hot, and shaking . . . so I told you I had a fever. You believed me. But you still sent me to sleep in the other room with the children. What a bastard.' She falls silent, out of dread, or decency. A blush appears on her cheeks, and spreads slowly to her neck. Her gaze is concealed behind dreamily closing eyelids.

She stands up, buoyant. 'Right, I must be going. My aunt and the children must be worried!'

Before leaving, she fills the drip bag with sugar-salt solution, covers her man, closes the doors and disappears into her veil, into the street.

The room, the house, the garden, all of it, buried in fog, disappears beneath that sad grey mantle.

Nothing happens. Nothing moves, except the spider which for a while now has been living in the rotting ceiling beams. It is slow. Slothful. After a brief tour of the wall, it returns to its web.

Outside:
 They shoot awhile.
 Pray awhile.
 Are silent awhile.

At dusk, someone knocks on the door to the passage.
 No voice invites him in.

He knocks again.

No hand opens the door to him.

He leaves.

Night comes, and goes again. Taking the clouds and the fog with it.

The sun is back. Its rays of light return the woman to the room.

After glancing around the space she pulls a new drip bag and a new bottle of eye drops from her bag. Goes straight over to the green curtain and draws it aside so she can see her man. His eyes are half-open. She pulls the tube out of his mouth, takes a cushion from under his head, and inserts the drops into his eyes. One, two; one, two. Then, she leaves the room and returns with the plastic basin full of water, a towel and some clothes. She washes her man, changes his clothes and settles him back into his spot.

Carefully she rolls up his sleeve and wipes the crook of his arm. Inserts the tube, fills the dropper correctly, and then leaves, carrying everything she must remove from the room.

We hear her doing the washing. She hangs it out in the sun. Returns with a broom. Brushes off the kilim, the mattresses . . .

She hasn't yet finished her task when someone knocks at the door. She walks to the window in a cloud of dust. 'Who is it?' Again the silent shape of the boy, wrapped in his *patou*. The woman's arms fall wearily to her sides. 'What do you want now?' The boy holds out a few notes. The woman doesn't move. Doesn't say a word. The boy heads for the passage. The woman comes out to meet him. They murmur a few inaudible words to each other and slip into one of the rooms.

To start with, there is only silence, then gradually some whispering . . . and eventually a few muffled groans. Then once again silence. For quite a while. Then a door opening. And footsteps rushing outside.

As for the woman, she goes into the toilet, washes herself and returns shyly to the room. Finishes her cleaning, and leaves.

Her footsteps ring out on the tiled floor of the kitchen, accompanied after a while by the hum of gas, spreading its sonic layer around the house.

Once she has made her lunch, she comes to eat it in the room, straight out of the pan.

She is soft and serene.

After the first mouthful, she suddenly says, 'I feel sorry for that boy! But that isn't why I let him in . . . Anyway, I hurt his feelings today, and almost drove the poor thing away! I got the giggles, and he thought I was laughing at him . . . which of course I was, in a way . . . But it was my fiendish aunt's fault! She said something awful last night. I'd been telling her about this stammering boy, and how he comes so quickly. And . . .' She laughs, a very private, silent laugh. 'And she said I should tell him . . .' The laugh, noisy this time, interrupts her again. ' . . . Tell him to fuck with his tongue and talk with his dick!' She guffaws, wiping away tears. 'It was terrible of me to think of that right then . . . but what could I do? As soon as he started stammering, my aunt's words flashed into my mind. And I laughed! He panicked . . . I tried to control myself . . . but I couldn't. It just got worse . . . but luckily,' she pauses, 'or unluckily, my thoughts suddenly took a different turn . . .' She pauses again. 'I thought of you . . . and suddenly stopped laughing. Otherwise it could have been a disaster . . . one mustn't hurt young men . . . mustn't take the piss out of their thing . . . They associate their virility with a long, hard dick, with how long they can hold back, but . . .' She bypasses that thought. Her cheeks are all red. She takes a deep breath. 'Anyway, it's over . . . but that was a narrow escape . . . again.'

She finishes her lunch.

After taking her pan back to the kitchen, she returns and stretches out on the mattress. Hides her eyes in the crook of her arm and lets a long, thoughtful moment of silence go by before confessing some more: 'So yes, that boy made me think of you again. And once again I can confirm that he's just as cack-handed as you. Except that he's a beginner, and a quick learner! Whereas you never changed. At least with him I can tell him what to do and how to do it. If I'd asked all that of you . . . my God! I'd have got a broken nose! And yet it's not difficult . . . you just have to listen to your body. But you never listened to it. You guys listen to your souls, and nothing else.' She sits up and shouts fiercely at the green curtain: 'And look where your soul has got you! You're a living corpse!' She moves closer to the hiding place: 'It's your blasted soul that's pinning you to the ground, my *sang-e sabur*!' She takes a deep breath: 'And it's not your stupid soul that's protecting me now, that's for sure. It's not your soul that's feeding the kids.' She pulls the curtain aside. 'Do you know the state of your soul right now? Where it is? It's right there, hanging above you.' She gestures at the drip bag. 'Yes, it's there, in that sugar-salt solution, and nowhere else.' She puffs out her chest: '*My soul feeds my honour; my honour protects my soul.* Bullshit! Look, your honour has been screwed by a sixteen-year-old kid! Your honour is screwing your soul!' She grabs his hand, lifts it up. 'Now, it's your body's turn to judge you,' she says. 'It is judging your soul. That's why you're not in physical pain. Because it's your soul that's suffering. That suspended soul, which sees everything, and hears everything, and cannot react at all, because it no longer controls your body.' She lets go of the hand and it falls back on to the mattress with a thud. A stifled laugh pushes her towards the wall. She doesn't move. 'Your honour is nothing more than a piece of meat, now! You used to use that word yourself. When you wanted me to cover up, you'd shout, *Hide your meat!* I was a piece of meat,' into which you could stuff your dirty dick. Just to rip it apart, to make it bleed!' She falls silent, out of breath.

Then suddenly she stands up. Leaves the room. She can be heard pacing up and down the passage, saying, 'What's the matter with me now? What am I saying? Why? Why? It's not normal, not normal at all . . .' She comes back in. 'This isn't me. No, it isn't me talking . . . it's someone else, talking through me . . . with my tongue. Someone has entered my body . . . I am possessed. I really do have a demon inside me. It's she who is speaking. She who makes love with that boy . . . she who takes his trembling hand and puts it on my breasts, on my belly, between my thighs . . . all of that is her! Not me! I need to get rid of her! I should go and seek counsel from the Hakim, or the Mullah, and tell them everything. So they can drive away this demon lurking inside me! . . . My father was right. That cat has come to haunt me. It was the cat that made me open the door to the quail's cage. I am possessed, and have been for years!' She flings herself into the man's hiding place, sobbing. 'This is not me talking! . . . I am under the demon's spell . . . this isn't me . . . where is the Koran?' Panicked. 'The demon has even stolen the Koran! The demon did it! . . . And the damned feather . . . she took that too.'

She rummages around under the mattresses. Finds the black prayer beads. 'Allah, you're the only one who can banish this demon, *Al-Mu'akhkhir, Al-Mu'akhkhir . . .*' She tells the prayer beads, '*Al-Mu'akhkhir . . .*', picks up her veil, '*Al-Mu'akhkhir . . .*', leaves the room, '*Al-Mu'akhkhir . . .*', leaves the house, '*Al-Mu'akhkhir . . .*'

She can no longer be heard.

She does not return.

As twilight falls, somebody walks into the courtyard and knocks on the door to the passage. No one replies; no one opens. But, this time, the intruder seems to stay in the garden. The sound of cracking wood, and of stones being bashed together, floods through the walls of the house. He must be taking something. Or destroying. Or building. The woman will find out tomorrow, when she returns along with the first rays of sunlight shining through the holes in the yellow and blue sky of the curtains.

Night falls.

The garden goes dark. The intruder goes off.

Day breaks. The woman returns.

Very pale, she opens the door to the room and pauses a moment to check for the slightest sign of a visit. Nothing. Distraught, she walks into the room and up to the green curtain. Pulls it slowly aside. The man is still there. Eyes open. The same rhythm to his breathing. The drip bag is half empty. The drops are falling, as before, to the rhythm of the breath, or of the black prayer beads passing through the woman's fingers.

She lets herself fall on to the mattress. 'Did somebody repair the door on to the street?' She is asking the walls. In vain. As always.

She picks herself up, walks out of the room and, still bewildered, checks the other rooms, and the cellar. She comes back up the stairs. Into the room. Confounded. 'But no one has been here!' She collapses on the mattress, in the grip of a growing weariness.

No more words.

No more movement, except the telling of the prayer beads. Three cycles. Two hundred and ninety-seven beads. Two hundred and ninety-seven breaths. No mention of any of the names of God.

Before embarking on a fourth cycle, she suddenly starts talking. 'This morning, my father came to see me again . . . but this time to accuse me of having stolen the peacock feather he used as a bookmark in his Koran. I was horrified. He was furious. I was scared.' The fear is still visible in her gaze as it seeks shelter in the corners of the room. 'But that was a long time ago . . .' Her body sways. Her voice becomes definite: 'It was a long time ago that I stole it.' She stands up suddenly. 'I'm raving!' she murmurs to herself, calmly at first, then fast, nervously. 'I'm raving. I've got to calm down. Got to stop talking.' She can't stay in one place. Keeps moving around, chewing on her thumb. Her eyes dart around frenetically. 'Yes, that fucking business with the feather . . . that's what it is. That's what is driving me crazy. That bloody peacock feather! It was only a dream, to start with. Yes, a dream, but such a strange one. That dream haunted me every night when I was pregnant with my first child . . . I had the same nightmare every night. I saw myself giving birth to a boy, a boy who had teeth and could already speak . . . He looked just like my grandfather . . . That dream terrorised me, it tortured me . . . The child used to tell me that he knew one of my biggest secrets.' She stops moving. 'Yes, one of my biggest secrets! And if I didn't give him what he wanted, he would tell that secret to everyone. The first night, he asked for my breasts. I didn't want to give them to him because of his teeth . . . so he started screaming.' She covers her ears with trembling hands. 'I can still hear his screams today. And he began to tell the start of my secret. I ended up capitulating. I gave him my breasts. He was sucking, and biting on them with his teeth . . . I was crying out . . . I was sobbing in my sleep . . .'

She stands by the window, with her back to her man. 'You must remember. Because you kicked me out of bed that night too. I spent it in the kitchen.' She sits at the foot of the curtains patterned with migrating birds. 'Another night, I dreamt of the boy again . . . This time, he was asking me to bring him my father's peacock feather . . . but . . .' Someone knocks at the door. The woman emerges from her dreams, from her secrets, to lift up the curtain. It's the young boy again. 'No, not today!' the woman says firmly. 'I am . . .' The boy interrupts her with his jerky words: 'I . . . m-m-mended th-the d-d-door.' The woman's body relaxes. 'Oh, so it was you! Thank you.' The boy is waiting for her to invite him in. She doesn't say anything. 'C-c-can . . . c-c-can I . . .' 'I told you, not today . . .' the woman says wearily. The boy comes closer. 'N-n-not . . . n-n-not to . . .' The woman shakes her head and adds, 'I'm waiting for someone else . . .' The boy takes another step closer. 'I . . . I d-d-don't w-w-want . . .' The woman cuts him off, impatient: 'You're a sweet boy, but I've got to work, you know . . .' The boy tries hard to speak quickly, but his stammer just gets worse: 'N-n-not . . . n-n-n-not . . . w-w-work!' He gives up. Moves away to sit at the foot of a wall, sulking like a hurt young child. Helpless, the woman leaves the room so that she can speak to him from the doorway at the end of the passage. 'Listen! Come this afternoon, or tomorrow . . . but not now . . .' Calmer now, the boy tries again: 'I . . . want t-t-to . . . s-s-speak . . . t-t-to you . . .' In the end, the woman gives in.

They go inside and ensconce themselves in one of the rooms.

Their whispers are the only voices echoing through and underlining the gloomy atmosphere engulfing the house, the garden, the street and even the city . . .

At a certain point, the whispering stops and a long silence ensues. Then suddenly, the violent slamming of a door. And the boy's sobs departing down the passage, across the courtyard, and finally fading into the street. Then the woman's furious footsteps as she marches into the room yelling, 'Son of a bitch! Bastard!' She stomps around the room several times before sitting down. Very pale. 'To think that son of a bitch dared spit in my face when I told him I was a whore!' she continues with rage. She stands up. Voice and body stiff with contempt. Walks towards the green curtain. 'You know that guy who came here the other day with that poor boy, and called me every name under the sun? Well, guess what he does himself?' She kneels down in front of the curtain. 'He keeps that poor little boy for his own pleasure! He kidnapped him when he was still a small child. An orphan, left to cope on his own on the streets. Kidnapped him and put a Kalashnikov in his hands, and bells on his feet in the evenings. He makes him dance. Son of a bitch!' She withdraws to the foot of the wall. Takes a few deep breaths of this air heavy with the smell of gunpowder and smoke. 'The boy's body is black and blue! He has burn scars all over – on his thighs, his buttocks . . . It's an outrage! That guy burns him with the barrel of his gun!' Her tears tumble on to her cheeks, flow down the lines that surround her lips when she cries, and stream over her chin, down her neck and on to her chest, the source of her howls. 'The wretches! The scoundrels!'

She leaves.

Without saying anything.

Without looking at anything.
Without touching anything.

She doesn't come back until the next day.

Nothing new.
    The man – her man – is still breathing.
    She refreshes the drip.
    Administers the eye drops: one, two; one, two.
    And that's all.

She sits down cross-legged on the mattress. Takes a
piece of fabric, two small blouses and a sewing kit
out of a plastic bag. Rummages in the kit for a pair
of scissors. Cuts up bits of fabric to patch the blouses.
    From time to time, she glances surreptitiously at
the green curtain, but more often her eyes turn
anxiously towards the curtains with the pattern of
migrating birds, which have been pulled open a crack
to make the courtyard visible. The slightest noise
draws her attention. She looks up to check whether
or not someone is arriving.
    And no, nobody comes.

As every day at noon, the Mullah makes the call
to prayer. Today, he preaches the revelation: '*Recite*

in the name of your Lord who created, created man from clots of blood. Recite! Your Lord is the Most Bountiful One, who by the pen taught man what he did not know. My brothers, these are the first verses of the Koran, the first revelation given to the prophet by the angel Gabriel . . .' The woman pauses and listens carefully to the rest: '. . . at the time Allah's messenger withdrew to meditate and pray in the cave of Learning, deep in the mountain of Light, our prophet was unable to read or to write. But with the aid of these verses, he learnt! Our Lord has this to say about his messenger: *He has revealed to you the Book with the Truth, confirming the scriptures which preceded it; for He has already revealed the Torah and the Gospel for the guidance of mankind . . .*' The woman goes back to her sewing. The Mullah continues: '*Muhammad is no more than an apostle; other apostles have passed away before him . . .*' Once again, the woman stops her patching and concentrates on the words of the Koran: 'Muhammad, our prophet, says this, *I have not the power to acquire benefits or to avert evil from myself, except by the will of God. Had I possessed knowledge of what is hidden, I would have availed myself of much that is good and no harm would have touched me . . .*' The woman doesn't hear the rest. Her gaze wanders among the folds of the blouses. After a long moment, she lifts her head and says dreamily, 'I have heard those words before, from your father. He always used to recite that passage to me, it amused him hugely. His eyes would shine with mischief. His beard would tremble. And his voice would flood that sweaty little room. He would tell me this: *One day, after meditating, Muhammad, peace be upon him, leaves the mountain and goes to his wife Khadija to tell her, "Khadija, I am about to lose my mind." "But why?" his wife asks. And he replies, "Because I observe in myself the symptoms of the insane. When I walk down the street I hear voices emanating from every stone, every wall. And during the night, a massive being appears to me. He is tall. So tall. He stands on the ground but his head touches the sky. I do not know him. And each time, he comes towards me as if to grab me." Khadija comforts him, and asks him to tell her the next time the being appears. One day, in the house with Khadija, Muhammad cries, "Khadija, the being has appeared. I can see him!" Khadija comes to him, sits down, clasps him to her breast and asks, "Do you see him now?" Muhammad says, "Yes, I see him still." So Khadija uncovers her head* and her hair and asks again, "Do you see him now?" Muhammad replies, "No, Khadija, I don't see him any more." And his wife tells him, "Be happy, Muhammad, this is not a giant djinn, a diw, it's an angel. If it was a diw, it would not have shown the slightest respect for my hair and so would not have disappeared." And to this, your father added that the story revealed Khadija's mission: to show Muhammad the meaning of his prophecy, to disenchant him, tear him from the illusion of devilish ghosts and shams . . . She herself should have been the messenger, the Prophet.'

She stops and sinks into a long, thoughtful silence, slowly resuming her patching of the little blouses.

She does not emerge from this silence until she pricks her finger with the needle, and shrieks. She sucks the blood and goes back to her sewing. 'This morning . . . my father came into my room again. He was holding a Koran under his arm, my copy, the very same one I had here . . . yes, it was he who took it . . . and so he had come to ask me for the peacock feather. Because it was no longer inside the Koran. He said it was that boy – the one I let come here, into my home – who stole the feather.

And that if he comes I must make sure to ask him for it.' She stands up, goes to the window. 'I hope he does come.'

She steps out of the house. Her footsteps cross the courtyard, stop behind the door that opens on to the road. No doubt she takes a quick look into the street outside. Nothing. Silence. No one, not even the shadow of a passer-by. She turns away. Waits outside, in front of the window. Silhouetted against the background of migrating birds frozen mid-flight on the yellow and blue sky.

The sun is setting.
   The woman must go back to her children.
   Before leaving the house, she stops by the room to carry out her usual tasks.
   Then leaves.

Tonight, they are not shooting.
   Beneath the cold, dull light of the moon, the stray dogs are barking in every street of the city. Right through till dawn.
   They are hungry.
   There are no corpses tonight.

As day breaks, someone knocks on the door to the street, then opens it and walks into the courtyard. Goes straight to the door into the passage. Places something on the ground and leaves.

As the last drip of solution makes it into the dropper and flows down the tube into the man's veins, the woman returns.

She walks into the room, looking more exhausted than ever. Her eyes are guarded, sombre. Her skin pale, muddy. Her lips less fleshy, less bright. She throws her veil into a corner and walks over, carrying a red and white bundle with an apple blossom pattern. She checks the state of her man. Talks to him, as she always does. 'Someone came by again, and left this bundle at the door.' She opens it. A few grains of toasted wheat, two ripe pomegranates, two pieces of cheese and, wrapped in paper, a gold chain. 'It's him, it's the boy!' An ephemeral happiness flits across her sad face. 'I should have rushed. I hope he comes back.'

As she changes the man's sheet: 'He will come back . . . because before he dropped by here, he came to see me at my aunt's house . . . while I was in bed. He came very gently, without a sound. He was dressed all in white. He seemed very pure. Innocent. He was no longer stammering. He had come to explain to me why that fucking peacock feather was so important to my father. He told me it was from the peacock that had been banished from Eden alongside Eve. Then he left. He didn't even give me a chance to ask him anything.' She changes the drip bag, adjusts the timing of the drops, and sits down next to her man. 'I hope you don't hate me for talking to you about him and entertaining him here in the house. I don't know what's going on, but he's very – how can I say? – very present for me. It's almost the same feeling I used to have about you, at the beginning of our marriage. I don't know why! Even though I know that he too could become awful, like you. I'm sure of it. The moment you possess a woman, you become monsters.' She stretches out her legs. 'If you ever come back to life, ever get back on your feet, will you still be the same monster you were?' A pause, as she follows her train of thought. 'I don't think so. I convince myself that you will be changed by everything I'm telling you. You are hearing me, listening to me, thinking. Pondering . . .' She moves closer to him. 'Yes, you'd change, you'd love me. You'd make love to me as I want to be made love to. Because now you have learned lots of new things. About me, and about yourself. You know my secrets. From now on, those secrets are inside you.' She kisses his neck. 'You'd respect my secrets. As I shall respect your body.' She slips her hand between the man's legs, and strokes his penis. 'I never touched it like this ... your ... your quail!' She laughs. 'Can you ...?' She slips her hand inside the man's trousers. Her other hand drops between her own thighs. Her lips skim over the beard; they brush against the half-open mouth. Their breath merges, converges. 'I used to dream of this ... always. As I touched myself, I would imagine your cock in my hands.' Little by little the gap between her breaths becomes shorter, their rhythm speeds up, overtakes the man's breathing. The hand between her legs strokes gently, then quickly, intensely ... Her breathing becomes more and more rough. Panting. Short. Heavy.

A cry.

Moans.

Once again, silence.

Once again, stillness.

Just breathing.

Slow.

And steady.

A few breaths later.

A stifled sigh suddenly breaks the silence. The woman says 'Sorry!' to the man, and shifts a little. Without looking at him, she pulls away and moves out of the hiding place to sit against the corner of the wall. Her eyes are still closed. Her lips are still trembling. She is moaning. Gradually, words begin to emerge: 'What's got into me now?' Her head bangs against the wall. 'I really am possessed . . . Yes, I see the dead . . . people who aren't there . . . I am . . .' She pulls the black prayer beads from her pocket. 'Allah . . . What are you doing to me?' Her body rocks back and forth, slowly and rhythmically. 'Allah, help me to regain my faith! Release me! Rescue me from the illusion of these devilish ghosts and shams! As you did with Muhammad!' She stands up suddenly. Paces around the room. Into the passage. Her voice fills the house. 'Yes . . . he was just one messenger among others . . . There were more than a hundred thousand like him before he came along . . . Whoever reveals something can be like him . . . I am revealing myself . . . I am one of them . . .' Her words are lost in the murmur of water. She is washing herself.

She comes back. Beautiful, in her crimson dress embroidered with a few discreet ears and flowers of corn at the cuffs and hem.

She returns to her spot next to the hiding place. Calm and serene, she starts speaking: 'I didn't go and seek counsel from the Hakim, or the Mullah. My aunt forbade me. She says I'm not insane, or possessed. I'm not under the spell of a demon. What I'm saying, what I'm doing, is dictated by the voice from on high, is guided by that voice. And the voice coming out of my throat is a voice buried for thousands of years.'

She closes her eyes and, three breaths later, opens them again. Without moving her head, she glances all around the room, as if seeing it for the first time. 'I'm waiting for my father to come. I need to tell all of you, once and for all, the story of the peacock feather.' Her voice loses some of its softness. 'But first I need to get it back . . . yes, it's with that feather that I'm going to write the story of all these voices that are gushing up in me and revealing me!' She becomes agitated. 'It's that fucking peacock feather! And where is the boy? What do I bloody want with his pomegranates?

Or his chain? The feather! I need the feather!' She stands up. Her eyes are shining. Like a madwoman. She flees the room. Searches the house. Comes back. Her hair a mess. Covered in dust. She throws herself on to the mattress opposite the photo of her man. Picks up the black prayer beads and starts telling them again.

Suddenly, she screams, 'I am *Al-Jabbar*!'

Murmurs, 'I am *Al-Rahim* . . .'

And falls silent.

Her eyes become lucid again. Her breath returns to the rhythm of the man's breathing. She lies down. Facing the wall.

Her voice gentle, she continues: 'That peacock feather is haunting me.' She picks a few flakes of peeling paint from the wall with her nails. 'It has haunted me from the beginning, from the first time I had that nightmare. That nightmare I told you about the other day, the child harassing me in my dream, telling me that he knew my biggest secret. That dream made me afraid to go to sleep. But the dream gradually wormed its way into my waking hours as well . . . I used to hear the child's voice in my belly. All the time. Wherever I was. At the baths, in the kitchen, in the street . . . The child would be talking to me. Harassing me. Demanding the feather . . .' She licks the tip of her nail, turned blue by the remnants of paint. 'In those moments all I cared about was making it cease. But how? I prayed for a miscarriage. So I could lose that bloody child once and for all! All of you thought I was simply suffering the same neuroses as most pregnant women. But no. What I am about to tell you is the truth . . . what the child said was the truth . . . what he knew was the truth. That child knew my secret. He was my secret. My secret truth! So I decided to strangle him between my legs, as I gave birth. That's why I wouldn't push. If they hadn't knocked me out with opium, the child would have suffocated in my belly. But the child was born. I was so relieved when I regained consciousness and saw that it wasn't a boy – as in my dream – but a girl! A girl would never betray me, I thought to myself. I know you must be dying to find out my secret.' She turns around. Lifts her head to look at the green curtain and slithers towards the man like a snake. As she reaches his feet she tries to meet his vacant eyes. 'Because that child was not yours!' She falls silent, impatient to see her man finally crack. As always, no reaction, none whatsoever. So she becomes bold enough to say, 'Yes, my *sang-e sabur*, those two girls are not yours!' She sits up. 'And do you know why? Because you were the infertile one. Not me!' She leans against the wall, at the corner closest to the hiding place, looking in the same direction as the man, towards the door. 'Everyone thought it was me who was infertile. Your mother wanted you to take another wife. And what would have happened to me? I would have become like my aunt. And it was exactly then that I miraculously bumped into her. She was sent by God to show me the way.' Her eyes are closed. A smile full of secrets pulls at the corners of her mouth. 'So I told your mother that there was a great Hakim who worked miracles with this kind of problem. You know the story . . . but not the truth! Anyway, she came with me to meet him and receive amulets from him. I remember it as if it were yesterday. All the things I had to hear from your mother's mouth on the way. She called me every name under the sun. She was yelling, telling me over and over that this was my last chance. She spent a lot of cash that day, I can tell you. And then I visited the Hakim several times, until I fell pregnant. As if by magic! But you know what, that Hakim was just my aunt's pimp. He mated me with a guy they had blindfolded. They locked us up together in the pitch dark. The man wasn't allowed to talk to me or touch me . . . and in any case, we were never naked. We just pulled down our pants, that's all. He must have been young. Very young and strong. But seemingly short of experience. It was up to me to touch him, up to me to decide exactly when he should penetrate me. I had to teach him everything, him too! . . . Power over another's body can be a lovely thing, but that first day it was horrible. Both of us were very anxious, terrified. I didn't want him to think I was a whore, so I was stiff as a board. And the poor man was so intimidated and frightened that he couldn't get it up! Nothing happened. We kept far away from each other, all we could hear was our jerky breathing. I cracked. I screamed. They got me out of the room . . . and I spent the whole day vomiting! I wanted to give up. But it was too late. The following sessions got better and better. And yet I still used to cry, after each one. I felt guilty . . . I hated the whole world, and I cursed you – you and your family! And to top it all, at night I had to sleep with you! The funniest thing was that after I fell pregnant, your mother was endlessly going off to see the Hakim, to get amulets for all her little problems.' A dull laugh rumbles in her chest. 'Oh, my *sang-e sabur*, when it's hard to be a woman, it becomes hard to be a man, too!' A long sigh struggles out of her body. She sinks back into her thoughts. Her dark eyes roll. Her ever-paler lips start moving, murmuring something like a prayer. Suddenly, she starts talking in a strangely solemn voice: 'If all religion is to do with revelation, the revelation of a truth, then, my *sang-e sabur*, our story is a religion too! Our very own religion!' She starts pacing. 'Yes, the body is our revelation.' She stops. 'Our own bodies, their secrets, their wounds, their pain, their pleasures . . .' She rushes at the man, radiant, as if she holds the truth in her hands and is giving it to him. 'Yes, my *sang-e sabur* . . . do you know the ninety-ninth, which is to say the last name of God? It's *Al-Sabur,* the Patient! Look at you; you are God. You exist, and do not move. You hear, and do not speak. You see, and cannot be seen! Like God, you are patient, immobile. And I am your messenger! Your prophet! I am your voice! Your gaze! Your hands! I reveal you! *Al-Sabur!*' She draws the green curtain completely aside. And in a single movement turns around, flings her arms wide as if addressing an audience, and cries, 'Behold the Revelation, *Al-Sabur!*' Her hand designates the man, her man with the vacant gaze, looking out into the void.

She is quite carried away by this revelation. Beside herself, she takes a step forward to continue her speech, but a hand, behind her, reaches out and grabs her wrist. She turns round. It's the man, her man, who has taken hold of her. She doesn't move. Thunderstruck. Mouth gaping. Words hanging. He stands up suddenly, stiff and dry, like a rock lifted in a single movement.

'It's . . . it's a miracle! It's the Resurrection!' she says in a voice strangled by terror. 'I knew my secrets would bring you back to life, back to me . . . I knew it . . .' The man pulls her towards him, grabs her hair and dashes her head against the wall. She falls. She does not cry out, or weep. 'It's happening . . . you're exploding!' Her crazed eyes shine through her wild hair. 'My *sang-e sabur* is exploding!' she shouts with a bitter laugh. '*Al-Sabur*!' she cries, closing her eyes. 'Thank you, *Al-Sabur*! I am finally released from my suffering', and embraces the man's feet.

The man, his face haggard and wan, grabs hold of the woman again, lifts her up and throws her against the wall where the khanjar and the photo are hanging. He moves closer, grabs her again, heaves her up against the wall. The woman looks at him ecstatically. Her head is touching the khanjar. Her hand snatches it. She screams and drives it into the man's heart. There is not a drop of blood.

The man, still stiff and cold, grabs the woman

by the hair, drags her along the floor to the middle of the room. Again he bangs her head against the floor, and then brusquely, wrings her neck.

The woman breathes out.
The man breathes in.

The woman closes her eyes.
The man's eyes remain wild.

Someone knocks at the door.

The man – with the khanjar deep in his heart – lies down on his mattress at the foot of the wall, facing his photo.
The woman is scarlet. Scarlet with her own blood.

Someone comes into the house.

The woman slowly opens her eyes.
The breeze rises, sending the migrating birds into flight over her body.

My thanks to

Paul Otchakovsky-Laurens
Christiane Thiollier
Emmanuelle Dunoyer
Marianne Denicourt
Laurent Maréchaux
Soraya Nouri
Sabrina Nouri
Rahima Katil

for their support
and their poetic gaze

www.vintage-books.co.uk